MASON'S LAW

AN ALEX MASON THRILLER

DAVID ARCHER

BLAKE BANNER

RIGHTHOUSE

ISBN-13: 978-1-63696-084-5

ISBN-10: 1-63696-084-7

Cover design by: Damonza

Printed in the United States of America

www.righthouse.com

www.instagram.com/righthousebooks

www.facebook.com/righthousebooks

twitter.com/righthousebooks

PRAISE FOR ALEX MASON

ALEX MASON THRILLERS
Odin (Book 1)
Ice Cold Spy (Book 2)
Mason's Law (Book 3)
Assets and Liabilities (Book 4)
Russian Roulette (Book 5)
Executive Order (Book 6)
Dead Man Talking (Book 7)
All The King's Men (Book 8)
Flashpoint (Book 9)
Brotherhood of the Goat (Book 10)
Dead Hot (Book 11)
Blood on Megiddo (Book 12)
Son of Hell (Book 13)

PROLOGUE

Aila Gallin killed the engine and the lights and watched the desultory raindrops slowly gather as amber globules on the windshield. They didn't seem to be in any kind of hurry. She slipped the small Sig Sauer P365 behind her back into her left-handed pancake, butt facing down, contrary to recommended practice. She climbed out of the anonymous, cream-colored 2010 Honda Civic and slammed the door.

She was on Old Queen Street. The name made her chuckle. She knew she had the sense of humor of a twelve year-old schoolboy, but she didn't care. She lifted her collar against the drizzle, shoved her hands into the pockets of her black leather bomber jacket and turned into Storey's Gate. The Westminster Arms pub was just forty paces away, painted shiny black with gold letters: the haunt of politicians, journalists and crooks.

She pushed through the door and was immediately struck by the warmth, the noise of conversation and laughter and the agreeable smell of beer. She scanned the room and saw Ahmed sitting at a table in the corner, ignoring a gin and tonic and looking at his cell phone. She elbowed her way to the bar, asked for a pint of best bitter and carried it to the table. He looked up as she sat.

"You're late."

"So is the Apocalypse, what can I say? Shit happens. Cheers." She raised her glass and pulled off a quarter of the pint. He didn't respond but settled back in his chair.

"You don't talk much like a rocket engineer."

She sighed, rolled her eyes, spread her hands and shrugged. "No. You're right. You know what? You're right. And my mother would agree with you. You know why?" He sighed and looked at the wall. She went on. "She would agree with you because, you know what she wanted me to be? She wanted me to be a good, Jewish wife, have five sons and for all of them to be doctors, lawyers and engineers. But it seems to be a curse I have, Ahmed, never to be what other people expect me to be. If I was the kind of person you expect me to be, I wouldn't be here right now talking to you, would I? I'd be in a lab somewhere, engineering rockets."

"Fine! OK, I have to be careful..."

She paused with the pint halfway on its return journey to her mouth. "You want me to start talking about vectors, thrust, parabolic arcs?"

"I said OK!"

She pulled off another quarter pint, smacked her lips and put the glass back on the table. Ahmed said, "You're Jewish."

"Jesus! Give the man a peanut! I just told you that, fifteen seconds ago. You think I don't know I'm Jewish? My parents reminded me every day of my life for the last twenty-eight years!"

"Will you please shut up?"

"Will you please say something intelligent?"

"We are trying to keep a low profile!"

"So I'm Jewish. What's your point?"

He leaned forward and spoke in a harsh whisper. "You're applying for a job with the Iranian government, the people who fund Hezbollah. How can you betray your country and your people like that?"

She stared at him for a very long moment. Her arched eyebrows and her tight mouth said she had lost hope of any kind of intelligent discussion.

"*My* country? *My* people? That piece of land belongs to the United States of America in all but name. And they did not steal it from us. They stole it from the Palestinians. And the people who live there are not my people. They are Russian, German, American, Palestinian, British, French—they are from the whole world, united by an idea that should have died out two thousand years ago! Me? I am English and I am not proud of it. I am ashamed of it. I am the daughter of a nation that has pillaged and plundered and stolen its way through twelve centuries of history. The people *I* have are my grandmother's people. She was a good, Palestinian woman, married to a Jew."

Ahmed frowned. "So you are a Muslim?"

"No. I am not a Muslim, I am not a Jew, I am not a Christian. I am not even a Buddhist or an atheist. I don't give a rat's ass about religion. I am a realist. I live here and now. And you know what the most important thing is, right now?"

He scowled. "Allah."

She gave a short, mocking laugh. "Money. You give me the money, and I will give you one of the best minds ever to come out of Cambridge University and the Massachusetts Institute of Technology."

"Your attitude disgusts me."

"And your teeth disgust me, Ahmed. But what can we do? Grin and bear it. Or in your case, please, just smile and bear it."

"If you talked like that in my country..."

"Yeah, I know. Tell me something I don't know, like what the salary is and when I start. You have my resumé, you've had time to check it out. So what's the deal?"

He took a piece of paper from his pocket and wrote a number on it. He slid it across the table to her. At first she thought it was a telephone number. She raised an eyebrow at him. "American dollars or British pounds?"

"Dollars. Don't get greedy. That is your fee over three years. You will be given accommodation and food. Payment will be made when you have finished the job."

"What guarantee have I got that you will honor this?"

"That is very simple. If you are successful we will want to use you again. Also, you will be useful to us installed in an American university."

"What university and what position?"

"I cannot be certain yet. Maybe Colorado. It cannot be too high profile. Your position will depend on what is available, but it will be a senior position."

She shook her head. "That is tempting, but there is no deal unless I get fifty percent upfront in an offshore numbered account."

"I will have to consult."

"That's crap and you know it. No one is going to accept the deal you're offering, Ahmed. Least of all if they have the kind of intellect you're looking for. You knew I'd ask for half upfront and you are ready to agree to that."

"I still have to report back. I cannot make that decision."

"OK, when do I start?"

"First of the month."

"Where?"

"You'll be given the details at the next meeting. Someone will inform you of the address."

"What about my expenses tonight?"

"What? You are joking!"

"Joking? You brought me out here in the rain to waste my time on this bullshit? No way, pal. Let's see how generous the Ayatollah can be."

He sighed and pulled two twenties and a ten from his wallet and tossed them across the table to her. She folded them carefully and smiled. "That's more like it." She drained her glass. "Pleasure doing business with you, Ahmed. How about a restaurant next time, and the Ayatollah buys me dinner?"

"Do not mock the Ayatollah. It will be bad for you if you do. The next meeting will be in a private house."

"Yeah, sure. Hang loose, dude."

She stood and pushed out of the pub without looking back. She lifted her collar against the steady drizzle and walked quickly back along Storey's Gate toward Old Queen Street. The only light was the limpid yellow from the tall, iron lampposts, which reflected wet and oily on the blacktop.

She climbed into her car, slammed the door, locked it and took a deep breath. Scanning her mirrors and finding nothing untoward, she took a transparent plastic bag from her glove compartment, folded the money and the note with her salary scrawled on it, and dropped them in the bag. Then fired up the engine and backed up illegally the hundred and fifty yards to The Two Chairmen pub, saying, "You got all that?"

Aaron's voice came back to her in the nano-speaker in her right ear.

"Affirmative. Where are you now?"

She spun the wheel so the car wound up facing west.

"On my way home. I'll drop the car at Oxford Street. Have someone collect it and give it a thorough cleaning."

"OK. Do you want company on the way home? Do you think they are buying it?"

She drove another hundred and thirty yards down Dartmouth Street to Tothill, chewing her lip. As she made a left toward Parliament Square she said:

"No, I'll be OK. I am pretty sure they are buying it."

She said it with more confidence than she felt. Ahmed was about as easy to read as Chinese algebra. Frankly, a little company on the way home in the form of four six-foot *katsas* seasoned in Krav Maga would have been reassuring. But she was playing a game she had to play alone. So she kept her eyes on her mirrors and drove.

At the Westminster Station Subway she turned left onto Parliament Street and Whitehall as far as Trafalgar Square, and there went five times around the circus to see if anyone had followed her. They hadn't, at least not in a car.

She made her way to Oxford Street and left the car at the

Oxford Street Multi-Story Parking Garage. She left the key in the glove compartment, made her way down to the crowded, wet street and walked round the corner to the Boots Chemist, where they sold just about everything from aspirin and saline solution to sandwiches and newspapers, by way of pens and wrapping paper. There she bought a large envelope which she addressed to a house in Washington DC, and stepped out onto the damp street again before dropping the transparent plastic bag containing the note with her proposed salary and the fifty pounds into the envelope.

From the Boots Chemist she hurried half a mile up Edgeware Road to the DHL office on the corner of Harrowby Street and pushed through the plate-glass doors. She handed over the envelope and told the Australian kid behind the counter:

"I need it there in twenty-four hours,"

He gave his head a twitch. "No worries. It'll be there."

"It had better be."

But she said that to herself, as she stepped out of the shop and into the rain, and scanned the street for a taxi. She saw the warm yellow light of a cab and raised her arm, emitting a piercing whistle at the same time. The cab swerved and pulled in, and she leaned in the window.

"Campden Hill Square, Holland Park."

They drove in silence. She watched the London streets move past, eternally wet, an ocean of bobbing umbrellas. It was a city she normally associated with safety and security, and homely common sense. But right then, riding through the dark among the millions of inhabitants that swarmed over its sidewalks and crammed into its roads, it seemed to her there was a madness that had infected the city; a craziness that somehow nobody else could sense. Because they all seemed to be possessed by it. All they could see was their wet feet pounding the wet sidewalks, the six feet in front of them as they pushed and elbowed and dodged through the crowds, tunnel-visioned into getting home to their TVs, where they would plug into the hive-mind, to be fed...

"What number, love?"

She snapped out of it and said, "Oh, right here is fine." She paid him, gave him a generous tip and pushed through the gate to the front yard of the elegant, four-story Georgian house. The path ran down the right side of the yard to the big, dark blue door with the big brass handle in the center. On the left were hedges and rosebushes. And dark shadows.

She fished her keys from her jeans' pocket as she walked. She slipped the key in the lock and paused. There was something, something she could not identify. She scanned the shadows, saw nothing, listened to the sounds behind the sound of the distant traffic. A rustle? A breath? But there was nothing. So why were the alarms going crazy in her head?

"I need a holiday," she told herself, and wondered about suggesting a couple of weeks in the Caribbean to Mason, as she pushed the door open and stepped into the hall. He might get the wrong idea. She smiled. That could be fun.

It was as she pulled the key out and closed the door with her foot that she realized what it had been—the noise. The key in the lock had sounded wrong.

She dropped, hunkered down and moved up against the wall. The house was absolutely silent. She pulled the P365 from behind her back and inched her way to the living-room door. It was open. She stood with her back pressed against the wall, listening for breathing. She heard nothing, moved in with the pistol held in front of her and smacked on the light. The room was empty.

She snapped off the light again and moved back into the hall, moving fast toward the kitchen. She made no effort to be silent. If there was anyone in the house they had already heard her switch on the living-room light. She kicked in the kitchen door, palmed the switch and nothing happened. Blackness. Her skin went cold and terror struck at her belly. She dropped to the ground and rolled and heard a heavy thud and a curse above her. Automatically she fired in the direction of the curse. There was a curse, "*Al'ama!*" a thud and a gurgle. Scuffling feet. The darkness seemed to shift. A boot stamped painfully on her leg. She bit back the scream of pain and swung savagely with the butt of her weapon, aimed blindly and fired again. A weeping, "*Allah!*" Then an arm like a vice around her neck. Hot, moist breath in her ear, "*Ya sharmoota!*" She couldn't breathe. She tried to twist the Sig behind her back, but a hand grabbed her wrist and levered the gun out of her fingers.

A savage voice in the dark: "*Kol khara!*"

Then a flash and an explosion, and darkness closed in.

JUST A QUARTER OF A MILE AWAY, in Ladbroke Square Garden, Aaron sat in the control car drumming his fingers on the wheel. For the fifteenth time he repeated, "Captain, come in please. Do you need assistance?"

Finally he took his secure cell and called the Chief at Russell Road.

"Yes."

"Sir, I have lost contact with the captain."

"What do you mean, lost contact?"

"She said she was going home. She left the car at Oxford Street. The car has been recovered according to plan. But I have been trying to contact the captain to confirm she has arrived home and there is no reply."

A sigh. "Perhaps she removed the earpiece."

"She would have notified me."

"Where are you?"

"Two minutes from her house."

"Come in. I'll send a car."

Aaron failed to suppress the note of anxiety in his voice. "Yes, sir," he said, and hung up.

ONE

Maria Garcia leaned forward into the candlelight. Her long, silver earrings hung down beside her long neck. A single pearl set among diamonds rested smugly in her perfect cleavage.

"This *is* the cognac talking," she said.

"It is very good cognac," I replied. "I can't wait to hear what it has to say."

"You're a bad man, Alex Mason."

"Come! That's the cognac talking."

"Be serious. I have always felt very drawn to you. I have fought against it, but it's an itch that just won't seem to go away."

"You must scratch, Maria. It's the only thing to do."

"Take me home, to your place, and scratch me. Do very, very bad things to me, Alex."

Coming from a woman who would send most supermodels crying back to Mommy, it was an offer I could not refuse. Except at that very moment, my cell vibrated in my pocket. It had to be the office because only the office had that number. My other phone I had deliberately left at home, so as not to be disturbed.

I ignored the vibration and signaled the waiter for the bill. It vibrated again. I leaned forward and breathed in her ear, "I'll be right back." And made my way to the bathroom.

Checking my teeth in the mirror, I asked severely into the cell, "What?"

It was not Lovelock. It was the Chief. "Be in my office in ten minutes."

"Sir, I am not only well over half an hour from your office, I am dining with the most desirable, carnal woman on the planet. And she likes me!"

A snort of amusement. "She won't like you that much when you tell her you have to go to the office, will she?"

"That's funny, sir. I didn't know you had a sense of humor."

But he'd already hung up.

She sat in the far corner of the cab and stared out the window all the way to her apartment. Once there she closed the door with unnecessary force and didn't say goodnight.

"Seventeen-oh-one, Fort Myer Drive," I told the driver and settled back in the cab to consider the magnitude of my loss.

I was still considering the magnitude of my loss when I settled myself into the leather armchair opposite the Chief, in his office on the eighteenth floor of the Commonwealth Building on Wilson Boulevard, in Arlington, Virginia. We watched each other for a moment and finally he took a deep breath and sighed.

"Sex is not good for you," he announced, massively. "It

dissipates one's fibers and uses up one's vital energy. As a pleasure it is overrated. Caviar, Chateau Lafite-Rothschild, 2016—Left Bank, of course. An Armand de Brignac Gold, brut."

"Sir, I dearly hope you did not call me here to discuss food and wine."

He shook his vast head. "No. I was merely trying to console you. I am going to send you to Iran. You will be impersonating a rocketry engineer, specializing in delivery systems for nuclear warheads."

The facetious humor drained out of me, leaving my skin feeling cold and pasty.

"They have warheads?"

"That is something I need you to confirm. However, everything seems to be pointing in that direction. What we could get, before our informant was silenced, was that there is a camouflaged laboratory-cum-facility in the desert to the south of Tehran..."

"Nine-tenths of Iran is to the south of Tehran."

"...thank you—where they have been working around the clock on developing nuclear devices for deployment against Israel. It also seems the device, or devices, in question are nearing completion." He shrugged. "Or have been completed."

"And you want me to infiltrate the lab?"

"That is the general idea. It won't be as difficult as it might at first appear. It seems the lab was recently subjected to a purge. Several of the scientists and technicians were suspected of working for Mossad or being Israeli sympathizers, or drawing pictures of people or something. Several of them were rounded up and marched off, and presumably tortured and killed. This may have put the authorities' minds at rest, but it also left them shorthanded."

"Particularly in the warhead delivery department, I gather."

"Precisely. So Iran has been quietly fishing in Western waters, looking for rocket engineers with certain, very specific qualifications."

"Such as?"

"Rampant, unbridled anti-Semitism, for a start, sympathy with the Palestinian cause, a desire to acquire a very substantial amount of money, and above all, a degree of proven skills in the field of delivery systems for nuclear devices."

"I am struggling to see how I tick any of those boxes, sir."

"That's irrelevant. We will provide you with a credible résumé from MIT, and any phone calls directed to them about your background will be redirected to us."

"I am guessing I don't have to send them my resumé and apply for an interview."

He sighed. "No, Alex, we have arranged a meeting in London with an Iranian agent who is making discreet inquiries on the Ayatollah's behalf. You will go there and have an interview with him. On the face of it, it will all be very much above board and legitimate. The Iranian government is looking for talented scientists and technicians to work in Tehran and help train Iranian engineers."

"Who's the agent?"

"Sir Leo D'Arcy of Croftmore—"

"Is that the Isfahan D'Arcys of Croftmore or the Rafsanjani D'Arcys of Croftmore?"

"It's an old Scottish family with a long history of service in the British army, and support for the Palestinians. Sir Jeremiah D'Arcy was vocal in the '40s against the recognition of Israel as a Jewish state. He was also notoriously sympathetic to Mosley and his Black Shirts—the British Fascist party. They are a long line of reactionaries who favor a strong link with the Arab nations."

"So my first meeting will be with this interesting gentleman."

"Yes."

"Will we be liaising with the Mossad on this? I believe the IDF has a pretty uncompromising line on Iran and nuclear weapons. They are committed to a preemptive strike as far as I am aware."

"They are indeed. We may liaise with them at a later date. Right now we are keeping this very much in house."

Something in his face made me ask, "Is Captain Aila Gallin involved, sir?"

There was a slight coloring of his cheeks, something I had never seen before. He also hesitated, which in my experience was also a first.

"Captain Gallin has been abducted and..." He hesitated again, working his lips soundlessly. "And, I am sorry, Alex, she is in all probability dead."

The room seemed to rock violently. We were quiet for a moment while I tried to assimilate the news. I heard him vaguely in the background saying, "I know you were fond of her."

I seemed to watch myself as though from far above, saying, "How did it happen?" Oddly. It seemed like a cold, meaningless question, as if how might matter. His voice seemed to come from another room. "I am not at liberty, Alex. I believe it was a home invasion. I can't tell you any more. I'm sorry."

"Was there a body?"

He shook his huge head. I can't..."

Goddammit, sir!" He glared at me. I insisted. "*Was there a body?*"

"No!"

"Blood?"

"Yes!"

"Is she dead?"

"I don't know, Alex! Do not ask me any more questions! The subject is closed!" He sighed again and repeated, "I am sorry. I know you were fond of each other. I know this must be painful. Go home. You will receive your briefing papers and identity documents in the morning."

I nodded. "Thank you, sir." I remained seated for another fifteen or twenty seconds. Then I stood and made for the door. His voice stopped me.

"Alex." I turned back. "You are under no circumstances to attempt to investigate her murder. It will jeopardize your mission and your life."

I nodded. "Yes, sir. I understand."

I left the building and stood on the sidewalk for a little longer than was normal, wondering what to do. I considered and dismissed a visit to a number of DC's late-night bars and instead walked down Wilson Boulevard searching for a cab to take me home.

In the cab I considered sending Maria Garcia a message, but—illogically—felt it would be an insult to Gallin's memory. So in the end I paid off the cabby, climbed the steps to my door and sat in my living room working my way through half a bottle of ten-year-old Bushmills, while Manny Pacquiao lay on my lap and allowed me to scratch his belly.

At four in the morning I made my way up to my bedroom and collapsed on my bed.

Morning came with a hangover. Made instantly worse by the appalling recollection of the news I'd received the night before. And, as I sat up and my stomach lurched, the bell started to ring downstairs. I ran down the stairs, fighting hard not to leave undigested, ten-year-old Bushmills on the stairs, and opened the door to a FedEx delivery man. He handed me a very large envelope, made me sign for it and left. I closed the door and ran for the bathroom.

A little later, over strong black coffee, eggs and bacon, I opened the envelope. As promised it contained my brief, a passport, driver's permit and a couple of major credit cards. My name was Dr. Henry Bassett, born in New York, graduated from MIT with a degree in Rocket Propulsion and later got a PhD from Caltech in Autonomous Remote Robotic Delivery Systems Deployed from Rocket and Jet-Propelled Platforms. I wondered if the acronym would be any easier, but gave up at ARRDSD...

There was some reading material on robotic delivery systems, so I'd have some idea what I was talking about at the interview, some family background and a thumbnail sketch of my personality, so I'd know how friends and colleagues, if approached, would describe me.

This was not something that had been prepared overnight, and that made me wonder if ODIN had been collaborating with the Mossad, and this had been what

Gallin was involved in when she was killed. It seemed likely, not least because my contact was in London, where Gallin was based. The Chief's refusal to discuss her death added weight to that possibility. The Mossad had told him they would take care of it.

It was as I was studying my brief over a second cup of coffee that the doorbell rang again. I peered through the spy hole in my door and saw it was a messenger from DHL. That made me suspicious, so I took the P226 from the drawer in the coat stand and slipped it into my waistband behind my back before I opened up.

"Yeah?"

"Are you Mr. Alex Mason?"

I slipped my hand behind my back like I had lumbar pain. "Yeah. You got something for me?"

"An urgent letter, sir. Can you sign here, please?"

I glanced at the envelope and saw it was from London. I signed, took the letter and carried it back to the kitchen. There I sat, opened the envelope and shook the contents out onto the table. There were two plastic bags. One contained a single slip of paper with a number on it. The other contained fifty pounds sterling, two twenties and one ten. I sat a long time staring at the items. I knew they were from Gallin. That much was obvious. There was no message, no indication of what the packages meant or why they were important.

That meant two things: she trusted that I would understand, and she was in a hurry. A real hurry. She was scared that she would be seen, or caught up with. She expected to be abducted or killed and she wanted me to—to what?

To have these items, clearly. Because they contained

information. What information could these papers hold? A number—a telephone number? It did not look like any code I knew, and it was a digit short. I glanced at the other plastic envelope. Money. Money! It was a bribe. A payoff? And the information contained on these pieces of paper was fingerprints. Paper is one of the best surfaces for recovering prints, and she had wanted me to know who had offered her the payoff. Because that was the person who had killed her.

I called Lovelock. Her disturbingly attractive voice answered.

"Yes, Alex. What can I do for you?"

"I need a messenger yesterday to take some items to the lab. I need fingerprints run through our database before this afternoon."

She was silent for a while, then: "On his way. Don't leave the house. What makes this so urgent? The lab will want to know why they are prioritizing it."

"It might tell us who murdered Captain Aila Gallin."

"Is that a priority for us?"

"Yes! And tell Nero I said so." Nero was the Chief's nickname, because he was said to set fire to things when he got mad. I went on. "We want to be friends with the Institute right now, and if we can help them on this they will be grateful. Make it happen, Lovelock."

She said she would and hung up. And I went upstairs to book a flight to London Heathrow, have a shower and pack.

―――

THREE AND A HALF thousand miles away to the north and the east, two men were also discussing Captain Aila Gallin.

One of them was Ahmed, the owner of the fingerprints on the note and the fifty pounds sterling that were about to be analyzed in DC. He was sitting, with his legs stretched out and his fingers in his jeans pockets, on a white windowsill in Kensington. Behind him the tall, sash window was open, overlooking a leafy crossroads with a triangular garden at its center. At that moment the man went by the name Ahmed, though he had so many false identities that sometimes he could not remember the name his mother had given him.

It had certainly not been Ahmed.

He had olive skin, pockmarked from a bad case of acne when he was sixteen, and large brown eyes which, for some reason, misled women into believing he had compassion. Right then, however, he was looking at Aaron Goldman, the young man in the chair across the room from him, with eyes that did not speak much of compassion.

"You tell me that she dropped the car at Oxford Street at seven thirty." He hunched his shoulders, bunched his mouth and nodded. "That is consistent—for London at that time of night—with her leaving the pub at seven. She has to walk to the car, drive up Whitehall, Trafalgar Square. Sure, that can take half an hour. But now you tell me that she got home at nine PM? You are telling me it took her *one and a half hours* to get from Oxford Street to Holland Park?"

"I had to pull back at Trafalgar Square. She is very smart. She'd told me she did not want company, and she went round the roundabout five or six times. If I'd stayed with her she would have spotted me. All I could do was go ahead and wait for her at the parking garage."

"And?"

"She went in, parked, and I waited for her to come

out. When she did she ducked into Portman Street, and by the time I'd turned and gone after her she was gone."

"Incompetence."

"I'm sorry."

"Your sorry does not help. What was she doing during that extra thirty to forty minutes? Was she abducted by aliens?"

Aaron Goldman had no answer, so he remained silent. Which made Ahmed scream at him, "*Answer me! Was she abducted by aliens?*"

"I don't know, Colonel. I imagine not."

"*But it is your job to know! That is why you were sent! So that you would know what she did!*"

"Yes, Colonel. I am sorry."

Ahmed's face flushed with repressed violence. "*So if it is your job to know and you don't know, then you are incompetent!*"

"I searched..."

"*Excuses!* One man in the car! One man on the street! It is basic technique!"

"Yes, sir, but I was alone."

Ahmed put his fingertips to his brow and closed his eyes. "Now, let me see if you are not too hopelessly mentally retarded for me to teach you something. If she disappeared for half an hour, forty minutes, where do you suppose she went?"

"I am not sure, Colonel. I thought probably she was just being careful."

The colonel nodded several times, with an insane light in his eyes. "Oh yes, oh yes, very good. So, let's see. Where do you suppose she assumed her prospective employer thought she was going?"

"...what?"

"In her mind! Put yourself in her mind! Where did she assume her employer thought she was going?"

"Home?"

"So, if she was being careful, why did she not just get a taxi *home?*"

"Uh..."

"*Because she wasn't going home, you jackass!*" He stared with bulging eyes at the younger man, who stared hard at the floor. The colonel shouted again. "*And she was not being careful! So where do you think she went?*"

"To...to..."

"To *co-mu-ni-cate!* She went to *co-mu-ni-cate to somebody!* And that means one thing, you stupid, moronic jerk! It means *she suspected the man she had spoken to! Me!*"

The moronic jerk babbled with bare, fragile coherence, "Yes, Colonel, I see that now. I am sorry. I will work very hard to learn these lessons and not fail you again."

Ahmed's voice was barely a whisper. "So whom did she contact?"

"Her father?"

"*No! Think!*" He thrust his face forward. "To communicate with her father she need only go and see him! He is a half-hour walk from her!" He sighed heavily. "Do you know why you are still alive, you wretched son of a bitch?"

The young man's cheeks flushed and tears welled in his eyes. He fought down the anger and the tears and said, "Through your compassion, Colonel."

The colonel shook his head. "No, because it would draw

too much attention to kill you now. But keep looking over you scrawny shoulder, sad little man. Stay alert. Now get out of my sight."

The younger man nodded and stood, fighting back tears of anger and hurt.

"I have been summoned back to Tel Aviv, sir. I fly this evening."

The colonel sneered. "Let's hope you're more use over there than you have been here."

"Yes, sir." He turned and left.

TWO

I touched down at Heathrow just before breakfast, collected my Avis F-Type Jaguar and drove through the English drizzle to the Dorchester. The English drizzle is something that the Brits hate. Personally I love it. It is like a perfect frame that brings out the beauty of every aspect of the painting. The hedgerows, the thatched cottages, the chimney stacks and the red busses. Even the shiny wet blacktop which they call tarmac acquires a special beauty in the drizzle.

I checked into my room overlooking Park Lane and Hyde Park and called a number Gallin had given me in one of her more human moments, while we were discussing what we should do if the other "didn't make it" while on a job. A gravelly, slightly confused voice said, "Yes, who is this?"

"Good morning, my name is Alex Mason, I am a friend of Aila's."

There was a long silence. "I know who you are. How did you get this number?"

"Aila gave it to me."

"Where and when?"

She had told me he would ask that, and I knew the answer. "Where? In her cups. When? Just after the ice had settled in Greenland."

A soft grunt over the line, and then, as though he were speaking with difficulty. "Why?"

She told me he would ask that, too.

"Because she was my friend."

Another, heavy silence and finally, "All right, Mr. Mason. You do not want me to grieve alone and in peace. A car will come for you in about twenty minutes. Try to be inconspicuous."

I had a quick shower, dressed inconspicuously in jeans and a blazer and went down to wait in the lobby, reading the *Daily Telegraph* in a large chair. After five minutes a guy in a suit pushed through the door. He was with a woman in a pretty dress who wouldn't stop talking and laughing. They headed for the bar, but halfway across the floor she stopped dead in her tracks and stared at me.

"Oh my god," she said. "Is it? I don't believe it! It is you, isn't it?"

I smiled blandly back. "It is certainly me," I said.

"Steve! Don't you recognize me? Oh, I am so *wounded!*" She laughed and came toward me, reaching for my hands. "Steve! It is so good to see you!" She turned and gestured toward the guy. "You don't know my fiancé, George Gallin, do you?"

By now I was on my feet. The message was subtle but

unmistakable. I shook George's hand and she kissed my cheek. "Say you'll have breakfast with us."

"I'd love to."

They bundled me out of the door and into a waiting cab, laughing and joking all the way. We pulled out onto Park Lane, circumscribed the whole of Hyde Park, went round the Marble Arch circus three times and then headed down past Notting Hill Gate toward the Shepherd's Bush circus. We went around that four times and finally turned into Holland Road, headed south toward Kensington High Street—all in total silence.

At High Street Kensington, they took a sharp right and a sharp right again and dropped me outside the Nox Hotel, on Russell Road.

"Go back seven doors. Ring the bell once. When they ask say it's Neil. Go. Fast!"

I got out, hunched my shoulders and looked at my feet as I walked down the wet sidewalk back the way we had come, toward High Street Kensington. As I went I counted seven front yards, then skipped up the steps to the door and pressed the bell. After a moment a deep voice asked, "Who is it?"

"It's Neil."

The door opened and there was a guy who looked like he'd been chipped out of concrete. He had a five-o'clock shadow and a cigarette that was too scared to give him lung cancer. He jerked his head like he thought words were for girls.

"Top floor."

"Thanks."

As I climbed I heard the volume of the TV increase and

decrease again before the living-room door closed. At the top of the stairs I knocked on a white door and a voice told me to enter.

Inside, the room was large. There were two tall sash windows which overlooked Russell Road. Directly in front of the door there was a desk. It stood at right angles to the window so that whoever sat there had a direct view of anyone entering Russell Road from Kensington High Street. To my left there was a nest of chairs and a sofa arranged around a coal fire burning in the grate. Sitting staring at the fire was a large, heavyset man in a charcoal gray suit. His face was dark and saturnine, with dark pouches under his brown eyes. He looked up as I closed the door.

"Mr. Gallin?"

His thick eyebrows rose high on his forehead. "She told you my name." His English was exquisite.

"Yes."

"She must trust you."

He didn't invite me to sit so I stayed standing by the door. I said:

"Trust is a rare commodity in our business. But we learned to trust each other."

"Trustworthiness is even more rare than trust. You had better sit down."

I sat opposite him. I put him in his late fifties, but you could tell he had aged in the last few hours.

"Forgive me, Mr. Mason, if I am less than polite. I would like to grieve in private. What is it you want?"

"I want to know what happened."

"Nobody knows what happened."

I shook my head. "That's not true. Somebody knows.

And I'll get to them in time. But right now I need to put together the little bit you know with the little bit he knows with the little bit she knows, until I have a picture that tells me something."

He frowned. "Is this you or ODIN?"

"Me."

"Does Nero know you are here?"

"Nero told me specifically not to look into this."

He looked away, back at the fire. "He was right. We asked him to stay out of it."

"I can't say I care."

"There is a greater fight. If we start putting our personal, emotional needs..."

I cut him dead. "What is the point of fighting to protect values, if we sacrifice those very values in order to defend them?"

He frowned. "What?"

"We risk losing sight of what we are fighting for, Mr. Gallin. Aila was my friend, maybe more than a friend. If I let her death go unavenged, unpunished, unanswered, then what the hell am I fighting for? To protect the military supremacy of a political entity, regardless, irrespective of its values?" I leaned forward and pointed at him. "I am not here to fight for my government, right or wrong. My government is charged with fighting for my values, come what may. And my values say that these bastards cannot come here and murder my friend, your daughter, and get away with it because it happens to be expedient for ODIN and the Mossad to let it slide. They will be punished, and I am going to punish them. So tell me, what happened?"

He surprised me by yawning and rubbing his face with

his hands, and I was suddenly aware that this was that yawn that comes so often with extreme grief, where your mind just wants to shut down and retreat into the dark, silent safety inside.

He groaned softly. "She trusted you," he said at last, and wiped his mouth with the palm of his hand. "You're the same kind of pain in the ass she was. This is unofficial, this conversation never happened and my advice to you is to obey Nero's orders. He is a wise and a highly effective man."

"Understood."

"We received intelligence that Iran was in the final stages of developing a nuclear bomb. It was a big shock to us. We keep a very close watch on Iran's nuclear program and we did not believe they were anywhere close to completing a bomb.

"Now we learn suddenly that friends of Iran, their agents in Britain, are looking for a rocket engineer whose specialization is delivery systems for nuclear devices. We hear that they have a bomb which is near completion, and now they are seeking a system to target Israel."

He watched me a moment, studying my face. "You knew this," he said and gestured at me. "I can see you knew this already."

"Our position has always been that if Iran develops a nuclear bomb, we will make a preemptive strike. This is a fight for survival. We will not—we *cannot*—hesitate."

He spread his hands, shrugged and sank back in his chair. "So it became imperative to find out for sure, to confirm, where they were at in their development, and stop them before it was too late."

"So Aila posed as a rocket scientist."

"Yes."

"And they didn't buy it."

"Apparently not."

"Who did she meet with?"

I was half expecting him to say, Sir Leo D'Arcy of Croftmore, but he surprised me by saying, "An Iranian going by the name of Ahmed. That was all we knew about him. They had been in touch and had one meeting, the night before last, at the Westminster Arms, by St. James's Park. She left that meeting at seven PM, deposited her car at the Oxford Street Car Park at half-past seven, according to plan, and then went off the radar until her backup called to say he couldn't raise her to confirm she'd got home safe."

"What time was that?"

"A couple of minutes after nine."

"That's a long time to get from Oxford Street to Holland Park."

"I raised the same question with him. He made a valid point. Aila is...or was, a very effective maverick. She operated her own way and her way was often—usually—the best way. And she deeply resented interference. He gave her a half hour's leeway before calling her. She didn't answer."

"Who was her backup?"

"You know I can't tell you that."

"I need to talk to him."

"I'll see what I can arrange. He is not in London now."

"What did you find at the house?"

He pointed to his desk. "The folder."

I stood and retrieved a manila folder from his desk. I handed it to him as I sat down. He opened it and leafed through several photographs which he handed to me.

"She was not there. There was no body. There were signs, in the kitchen, as you can see, of a scuffle. There was a lot of blood. The greater part was not hers." A grim smile touched his lips with pride. "But there were traces of her blood too. Of course that means nothing, except that her body was not at the scene of her abduction."

I studied the large, glossy prints.

"They took her away alive." I glanced at him. "They wouldn't clean up most of her blood and leave their own. Even if they killed her bloodlessly, it would still make no sense to take her body away and leave some of her blood and all of her attacker's. The only sense in taking her away would have been to interrogate her."

He closed his eyes and his skin became pasty. "It is almost preferable that they had killed her."

"Steady, Mr. Gallin. Try to keep perspective. I know it's not easy, but you know as well as I do that these guys will interrogate you either to make an example of you or to get information from you. And it's completely different in each case. Even these bastards know by now that information obtained under torture is not reliable. If they want reliable information, it won't be a picnic, but they won't be making an example of her either."

"You overlook the most likely scenario: that they have taken her simply to execute her. Do not delude yourself, Mr. Mason. The chances are she is dead."

"Why would they take her away to execute her?"

He was barely audible when he answered. "To make an example of her..."

I thought about telling him about the fifty pounds and the note, but he seemed to be coping with enough as it was. I nodded and stood. "Would you like me to keep you posted on what I find?"

He thought for a long time, staring at the fire. I was about to leave when he said, "If you can bring me my daughter back from the dead, let me know. Otherwise, let me grieve in peace and lay her to rest."

There was nothing I could say, so I left the room and went down the stairs into the mid-morning drizzle. My feet carried me back toward Kensington High Street. The cars and the red buses had their headlamps on in the dull, gray light, and there was a damp chill in the air that crawled up your ankles and down your neck. You could smell autumn creeping in, and on its tail was winter.

Around the corner I found a Costa Coffee, and as my cell started to ring I decided to push inside and have breakfast.

"Yeah, Mason."

"Hey, Alex, it's Caroline at forensics."

"Hello Caroline at forensics. Bear with me a minute, will you, I am just buying a coffee and some croissants." To the gap year student whom his employers insisted on calling a barista, I said, "I want four espressos in one cup, and I want two croissants. And I don't want them irradiated, please."

"You're like that with everyone, huh?"

"I'm even-handed."

"Are you going to sit down?"

The barista, or bartender, rung up the four coffees and the two croissants and I handed him ten English bucks.

"Yes," I said into the phone, which was now clenched on my shoulder. "Why?"

"Good. Tell me when you're sitting."

I took my meager change and my fare on a tray and weaved my way to a quiet corner where I sat. Then I took the phone in my hand and said, "So, tell me."

"You sent us the note and the English money."

"I knew that."

"So we isolated Captain Gallin's prints and looked at the fresh prints that were clearly on top of the rest. That would be the person who handled the paper immediately before she did."

"Right."

"Then we ran comparisons with the prints we took from the money and matched them to the prints on the note. OK?"

"So the guy who gave her the money is the same guy who wrote the number on the paper."

"Correct. Then we ran those prints through the Five Eyes database."

"And, did you get a hit?"

"Kind of."

"What does that mean?"

"It means we got a very special kind of hit. It was flagged and the Chief was notified automatically. He called the lab and wanted to know what the hell was going on and I had to tell him. He went ballistic."

"Well, who the hell was it? Who do the prints belong to?"

"Wait. I'll tell you, but I also have to tell you somebody else was notified of the hit too."

"Who?"

"I don't know. Some department attached to Five Eyes in the United Kingdom. But the identity was suppressed. It's a bit like caller ID withheld. But somebody in the UK knows we ran those prints."

"So are you going to tell me who the prints belong to?"

She took a deep breath. "In a word, no."

"Why the hell not?"

"Because they are contained in a file which is sealed. It is classified as top secret. From here I can't even see who *is* entitled to see it. Only people with top secret clearance."

"So the person who gave her that money and that note..."

"Probably works for either the Australians, the British, the Canadians, New Zealand or the USA."

I thanked her and hung up, and sat staring at my coffee and my croissants. Suddenly I had lost my appetite.

THREE

THE BREEZE WAS SALTY AND FRESH. IT SMELT clean, coming off the gleaming turquoise of the Mediterranean. It was occasionally blustery, flapping at the yellow awning of the Classic Café and rocking the parasol under which Sarah sat with her aunt.

"Isn't it beautiful, Aunt Peg? Mom would have loved it. She always wanted to come to the Mediterranean."

Aunt Peg's smile was more of a wince. "Yes," she said with little conviction. "But she was more about Rome, Italy...," she paused and added, "the Vatican," with some feeling.

"Do you know, Aunt Peg, that Beirut is the *oldest continuously inhabited city in the world?*"

"Well, it does look a bit run-down."

Sarah sighed, sipped her coffee and gazed out at the sea for a while. Eventually she said, "You don't like him, do you?"

Aunt Peg echoed her niece's sigh. "It's not that, Sarah, honey. He's real handsome, I'll grant you that."

"Those *eyes!* So cute!"

"Yeah, well, I always preferred blue myself. But it's all so...*foreign*."

"It's only foreign to us! It's not foreign to them! Is it?"

"Now don't get mad. I'm just saying. To *us* it's all foreign. We don't know where we stand, do we? They start talking and it's all *halal, halal halloumi*."

"Aunt Peg! Next thing you'll be telling me you voted Republican!"

It was Aunt Peg's turn to gaze out at the sea. Sarah frowned at her.

"He is actually a really smart guy. He has two degrees!"

"What in?"

"Medicine and law."

Aunt Peg arched an eyebrow, cleared her throat and kept her eyes firmly on the ocean. Sarah adopted a whining tone. "C'mon, Aunt Peg! I need you to like him! You've spoken to him. You know how smart he is. He knows *everything* about history! Did you know that this city was once a Phoenician citadel?"

It seemed to Aunt Peg that as an historian, Ali—the young man in question—knew a great deal about those hazy, indemonstrable areas of history that deal with America's imperialism in the Middle East. Her own recollection of history was that the Middle East and North Africa had been largely controlled by the British, the French and the Italians until shortly after the Second World War, when they had kicked everyone out and a few privileged families had seized the oil. But apparently the imperialism in question, he had explained to her with unsettling precision and a little too much passion, was the capitalist imperialism of corporate America exploiting the unfettered power of the Federal Reserve and funding the evil state of Israel and bringing poverty to the Arab people.

She had been about to observe to him that to an outsider, those parts of the Middle East where the poorest members of society drove cars most Americans couldn't afford, were the same ones not ruled by Islamic fundamentalists, and where people did not get murdered for watching TV. Plus, the only poor parts she *had* found were the ones where they were and they did. Did he think there might be a connection?

But a cautionary glare from Sarah had silenced her. She had limited herself to a smile and, "I was never great at history."

They had spent the better part of the week with him and by now Aunt Peg was fantasizing about boarding the plane the next day, and going home sweet home to Bridgeport, Connecticut, where she could forget all about Allah, Mohammed and American corporate imperialism. Not to mention Zionist, Masonic plots to rule the world.

She smiled to herself and thought of the Bernsteins at number one seventy-five. He was a gynecologist and she always brought a fabulous blueberry pie to the church garden party. She'd never thought about that before. It was Ali and his ranting about American Zionist imperialism that had brought it to mind. Mrs. Bernstein bringing blueberry pie to the church garden party. She smiled and chuckled to herself. Sam and Rachel conspiring to conquer the world.

"What are you laughing at?"

There was an accusation lying only partially hidden in her niece's tone. Peg forced herself to smile as though she hadn't noticed it. Keep the peace, she told herself. Tomorrow they'd be on their way home to peace and sanity.

"I was just remembering your mother. She was always the wild rebel. Dad couldn't handle her. They used to have the *most* ferocious rows. When she told him she was going to Woodstock he threatened to kick her out. She told him that just proved what a fascist he was."

"Gosh! I didn't know that."

"Well, considering he'd lost his right leg fighting the Nazis, it probably wasn't the smartest thing to say. But Mom had a talk with her and she did eventually apologize. Dad was authoritarian, but he was also pretty liberal for the times, and a good man. He was smart. Had his feet firmly on the ground. I miss him a lot. I miss them all."

They were silent for a moment. Then Sarah said, "Ali says..."

Aunt Peg reached across the table and placed her hand on her niece's arm. "Honey, do you think that for just a while we could talk about something that isn't Ali? I know you're in love with him, I know he has you all head over heels, but I am just a suburban, all-American girl next door, and I think if I hear one more thing about Allah or the wisdom of Mohammed, I might just explode!"

Sarah studied her fingers on the table before her for a moment.

"I guess I'm being a bit of a bore, huh?"

"You're allowed to be when you're in love. Maybe if you'd fallen for a blond, blue-eyed quarterback called Chuck

I wouldn't have found it so challenging. But I guess like your mom, you had to be different."

Sarah's face lit up and, not for the first time, Aunt Peg had the feeling she was talking to herself.

"Look! He's back!" She half stood and waved like an army wife welcoming back her husband after three months on the front line. "Ali! Ali! Over here!"

He strode onto the terrace where they were sitting at the back of the café, perched over the gleaming waves, and sat and smiled at them both. "Hello, Aunty, and Peg darling."

As she watched him, lean, hard and muscular, Aunt Peg could not help feeling there was something predatory about that smile. He winked at Sarah. "Did you miss me?"

Peg looked away at the waves while Sarah said, "Every moment," and they kissed for far too long, until Peg was forced to clear her throat. Sarah flopped her head on one side, clasping her heart and sighed, "Sorry, Aunty!"

And Ali regarded her with a smile that was nothing short of insulting. Peg made to stand.

"Look, perhaps you kids would rather be alone..."

"No!" It was Ali, wagging his finger. "No, you must stay. I want to become a good friend of Sarah's family. Please, forgive me, love has made me behave impolitely. I promise it will not happen again."

So she was compelled to stay, and her dream of stretching out on the bed and reading John Grisham's *The Judge's List* were shattered. She sagged slightly in her chair and Ali turned to Sarah.

"Darling, I want you to do me a favor, please?"
"Anything!"

What a surprise, thought Aunt Peg, *and there was me thinking she was going to tell him to go take a hike.*

"I have just come from my cousin's house. Cousin Suleiman." His eyes became suddenly moist. His head tilted to one side. "He has so many children. All day he is working, and at night he works too, to feed his children and give them a good home, thanks Allah. You do not know what this is like, in America. Everybody is rich there. Everybody has big house, big car, money." He rubbed his fingers and his thumb together and for a moment Aunt Peg thought she might hate him. He went on, "But he must fight and struggle like Americans do not know how. Now, his oldest son, Raza, has gone to United States and Suleiman is send to him a gift. It is a small, gold amulet that belonged to his father's great-grandfather, given to him by Imam Ali ibn Abu Talib. It is inscribed with the sacred words of the prophet."

"Oh, my *Gosh!* Aunty, did you hear that?"

"I'm sitting right here."

"I ask you, my angel, Sarah, I wish to entrust you with the sacred task of taking this treasure, the Word of God, Allah, and give it to Raza in New York. Will you do that for me, and for my cousin Suleiman?"

"Of course we will, my darling. We will, won't we, Aunty?"

He turned to her and again she could not fight the feeling that his smile was some kind of an insult. "You will help us in this, Aunty?"

She nodded. "On one condition." She pointed at Sarah. "You go back to calling me Aunt Peg, the way you have all your life, and cut out this *aunty* crap."

Sarah rolled her eyes. "Oh Aunt...Aunt *Peg*. My God,

you are so prickly! We *will* take this treasure to Raza, won't we, *Aunt Peg*?"

"We sure will." She turned to Ali. "Just give us his address and we'll get it to him."

"You must take in person to his house. Hand to him in hand, in person. You are now my family, Aunty. My blood is your blood. My home is your home. My food is your food. I thank you. May Allah's blessing go with you always wherever you walk. *Allahu Akbar!*"

Aunt Peg laughed and patted his arm. "Gee, thanks, but mostly I go by car. We'll gladly take it to him, so long as it's not in San Diego. Now, how about some lunch? I am *starving!* My treat."

Ali put his hands together like he was praying. "I have a small problem in my family, with Suleiman. I must go to him. But I will see you tonight and I invite you to dinner. I will give you the package for Raza, and of course I will drive you to the airport tomorrow."

He clenched Aunt Peg's hand, gazed at her with watery eyes, gave Sarah another long, lingering kiss and strode out of the café again. Sarah took a deep breath, held it and let it out as a heavy sigh.

———

GALLIN OPENED her eyes and felt a lurch of terror. She saw only blackness. Was she blind? She lay very still and felt about her. She was on a coarse blanket. There was no pillow. A wall on her left was rough and cold. On her right she felt the edge of the narrow bunk she was on. Carefully she sat up. She was barefoot and felt the cold, hard floor on the soles of her feet.

She explored her body with her hands and discovered that she was naked. Slowly she inched along the bunk to her left and at the end she found another wall. She stood with care, fighting to quell the panic that was stirring in her belly. Moving her palms along the wall, a foot at a time, her hip touched something cold, smooth and hard. She bent and with her right hand she felt its curve, a toilet, then a little higher, a basin, taps, and on the wall a small mirror.

She was in a cell. She froze and listened. Was she alone in the cell? She could not hear breathing. She could hear nothing.

Holding the basin, she moved another couple of sliding steps to her right and came to another wall. She calculated by the size of her steps that the cell was perhaps seven feet across. She now turned at the corner and began working her way carefully along the wall opposite her bunk. Aside from being rough, bare concrete, it was featureless and there was no furniture against it.

After about ten or twelve feet she came to another corner and here she felt the large, metal hinges of a steel door. She hammered on it with her fists and shouted, but received no response aside from the echo of the blows.

After a few more blows, she moved past the door, found the next corner and inched her way back to the bed. She found no light switch, no table, no chair.

In her gut she felt despair growing like twisted creepers out of her suppressed panic. Immediately she dropped and managed fifty push-ups, though her neck and shoulders cried out in bruised, strained pain.

She spent another hour doing warming and stretching exercises in the blackness. Then sat on the bunk in the lotus position and meditated to stabilize her emotions.

That was when she heard the metallic echo, and after a second feet tramping, growing louder as they approached. Relief flooded her belly as a thin strip of light appeared at the base of the door. They had not blinded her.

An iron key rattled savagely in the door. She grabbed the blanket from the bunk and wrapped it around her. The door opened and she saw the stark stencil of a man with two armed figures behind him. Then the light snapped on. She clenched her eyes shut and covered them with her right hand, while her left unconsciously gripped the blanket.

When she finally managed to force her eyes open, she saw a man in an expensive suit. His shirt had no collar, like a grandfather shirt, and he wore no tie. He had a black goatee and black hair brushed back. His nose was aquiline, and his eyes impenetrable.

Behind him stood two soldiers in combat uniform, holding Chinese AKM Type 56 clones. Panic threatened to well again. They were Iranians. She was in Iran. She stared at the guy in the suit and allowed herself to vent.

"What the *hell* am I doing here? What the *hell* is going on?"

He didn't answer her question. He folded his arms and said, "You are an Israeli spy."

She took all the resignation and hopelessness she felt right then and converted it into incredulous outrage. She squinted at the man like he'd just told her the world was flat.

"*What?* Are you out of your *mind?*"

"We have information. You are an Israeli spy."

"What you have is *bullshit!* You have *information?* Well let me tell you, your information is not only wrong, your informant is stupid! I come from a Jewish family, for Christ's sake! I was born a Jew! I am a high-profile scientist! Do you seriously think, with that kind of background, that I would become a *spy?*" He drew breath to speak, but she interrupted him, her voice rising and becoming shrill. "And if I did, do you seriously think I would have told you I was *Jewish?* I *have* an IQ of a hundred and fifty! That means I am *not* stupid!"

He turned and said something to one of the soldiers, who trotted away and returned with a bentwood chair. The man took it and sat.

"I do not want to hurt you."

"Yeah, good. Can I go home now?"

"But you have made a big mistake."

"No!" She shook her head vigorously and pointed at the guy in the suit. "*You* have made a big mistake. I am a scientist, a materialist and a selfish money-grubbing bitch. I don't give a damn about politics or religion. And I took Ahmed's offer because he *promised* me a lot of money. This is *bullshit!* This is *exactly* why I am not religious! I am a *scientist* and you need me on your program!"

"Be quiet."

She went silent but stared at him like she was going to cry.

"You are Mossad agent Aila Gallin, based in London. Your mission is to infiltrate the Iranian nuclear program and sabotage it."

She stared at him with squinting eyes, shaking her head. "I am *who?* You are out of your *mind!* That's fantasy. It's bad

Hollywood. You—Ahmed, you came to *me*. I never sought you out. Surely you must know that! And besides, if my father is to be believed, which he usually is, if Israel had the slightest suspicion that you had an atom bomb, they would not send a small, feeble, neurotic girl to infiltrate and sabotage you. They would just nuke you first!"

"Ahmed contacted you?"

"Yes!" She nodded a lot. "How the hell would I have known you were looking for a rocket engineer? He came to me and started talking religion to me. I told him I didn't give a damn about religion, I was an atheist and I didn't give a rat's ass about politics, either. He laughed, like he liked that, came to see me a few times at the campus, and then made me the offer. That is exactly how it happened."

"You say."

"Yeah, I say. And like I said before, I have an IQ of one fifty, and if I was a spy infiltrating your program, I would have made damn sure I had proof."

He sat for a long while, staring at her. Eventually he said, "You are a spy for the Mossad." He shook his head and sighed. "I do not believe you have any information of value to us." He shrugged and spread his hands. "You know what we do with Jewish spies?"

She allowed herself to start weeping. "What are you talking about? I am *not* a Jewish spy. This is *insane!*"

He leaned forward and smiled. "We shoot them." He turned to the guards and jerked his head toward her. They tramped in, grabbed her by her arms and dragged her out of the cell. She stumbled, the blanket fell from around her shoulders and they laughed and hurled insults at her as they shoved her down the stark, gray corridor.

FOUR

THE CALL CAME AS I WAS HAVING COFFEE AFTER A late lunch at the hotel.

"Is that Dr. Henry Bassett?"

"Speaking."

"My name is Strachan," he pronounced it *Strawn,* "I am the personal secretary to Sir Leo D'Arcy of Croftmore. He was wondering if you would care to dine with him this evening and discuss certain matters of mutual interest."

"I certainly would."

"Say, seven thirty for eight?"

"Seven thirty for eight."

"I'll have a car pick you up at seven."

We made extremely polite farewells and hung up.

I sat for a while, chewing my lip and wondering about the fingerprints on Gallin's note and the money, the members of the Five Eyes and Sir Leo D'Arcy of Croftmore. Was this one of those cases where the right hand doesn't know what the left hand is doing, and ends up shooting the left hand in the head? The possibility stirred a slow, hot burn in my belly.

What troubled me was that Gallin had not met with Sir Leo. It was not all that hard to imagine a scenario where the British Secret Intelligence Service set up a fake recruiting service for the Iranian nuclear program, with a view to penetrating the atomic bomb project, but failed to tell the Mossad about it. The UK's relationship with Israel, and particularly the Mossad, was sensitive to say the least. If Gallin had been on a mission similar to mine, she could have wound up on the wrong end of an MI6 executioner's Glock.

Logic would dictate that they would interrogate her and try to turn her instead of eliminating her. But that said, aside from the fact that Gallin could be pretty uncooperative when she wanted to be, there was also the issue of urgency. The Middle East could be balanced on the edge of a nuclear holocaust which would have devastating economic consequences for the whole world. So maybe the thinking at MI6 was to detect and eliminate any candidates applying for the job in Tehran, and slip their own man in instead.

Which raised the very ugly possibility that Gallin had been murdered so that I could get that job.

I sipped my coffee and realized it was cold. Cold as it was, it did nothing to stop the burning in my gut. So I went up to my room, showered and shaved, and dressed appropriately for dinner with a minor member of the aristocracy.

The car arrived promptly at seven. If I'd expected a Rolls I would have been disappointed. It was a twenty year-old Rover 75. It did, however, have a walnut dash and steering wheel, leather seats and a chauffer with a cap.

He took me to Launceston Place—pronounced 'Lawnsten Place' by the kind of people who find foreigners amusing—and dropped me outside a large, cream-colored house with two floors, a basement and a stoop. The door to the house opened as the chauffer opened the car door for me, and an elderly butler in a striped black and gray waist-coat greeted me as I climbed the steps and asked if he could take my coat and scarf. I told him he could and he led me across an ample entrance hall to a drawing room.

The room was not what I had expected. Given all the Old World trappings so far I had expected a lot of dark wood and burgundy leather. Instead it was expensive, Scandinavian minimalism, with lots of gray and beige calico, blond wood and abstract art on the walls. I was also surprised to see that the man I took to be Sir Leo D'Arcy was not alone. There was a woman in the room with him. She was in her fifties and still attractive in a mauve satin evening gown, seated on the calico sofa with a flute of champagne in her hand.

He was standing by a heavy oak credenza which might have been a Scandinavian antique, mixing a drink at a silver tray of decanters. He had silver hair and an excessively easy smile.

The butler said, "Dr. Henry Bassett, sir," and Sir Leo advanced on me with both hands held out toward me.

"My dear Dr. Bassett," he said with exaggerated warmth in his voice. "How do you do? So good of you to come at such short notice."

We shook, I muttered something about how it was kind of him to invite me, and he gestured to the woman watching us from the sofa.

"Allow me to introduce my wife, Lady Leila D'Arcy."

"How do you do?"

"I do the best I can," she said with a rich, husky voice and amused eyes. "How do *you* do?"

I couldn't think of a witty reply worthy of Bernard Shaw or Oscar Wilde, so I laughed like she'd said something funny and muttered something about "hangin' in there."

Sir Leo was retreating toward the drinks tray, talking over his shoulder as he went.

"Now, let me fix you a drink. What'll it be?"

"A martini would be fine."

"You must be wondering why a perfect stranger has invited you to dinner completely out of the blue!"

I smiled at his wife and said, "Not at all. Complete strangers invite me to dinner out of the blue all the time."

He pretended to laugh, repeated, "Excellent!" a few times and brought me my drink. "I just couldn't let the opportunity pass, I'm afraid. An acquaintance in the States heard you were coming over and called to let me know."

I frowned. "Either we have a mutual friend, Sir Leo, or you have a deep interest in rocket science. I can't think of any other reason why..."

Lady Leila scoffed and sighed loudly. "Leo! You are explaining it all wrong. You will have poor Dr. Basset thinking we are stalking him!" She turned to me. "It is a case of synchronicity, Henry—may I call you Henry? Dr. Bassett is not only far too formal, it makes you sound like a sad dog."

"You can call me Dr. Rottweiler if you like, but Henry is fine."

"I am Persian," she announced suddenly, as though the fact was somehow a reason why she couldn't call me Dr.

Rottweiler. "My parents were closely related to the Shah, and when the revolution came they were arrested and killed, and I was smuggled out to London with the Ayatollah's secret police just minutes away from catching me. I was very small at the time. A tiny baby in fact." She gazed with ill-concealed defiance at her husband. "Wasn't I, darling?"

"Barely out of nappies."

"Naturally, Leo and I are not supporters of the new regime. We do, however, retain friends over there, some of whom are in the scientific community." She laughed. "It is a sign of the brilliance of the Iranian regime that where modern technology is frowned upon by the imams, particularly satanic inventions like television which portray the human form, the use of nuclear science to make bombs with the potential to annihilate all of God's creation, is positively fostered."

I made the face of innocence. "But I believe their atomic bomb program is frozen, isn't it?"

I saw her eyes dart at her husband. "I am not up to date. Leo knows more about the political developments. I know only that the people who murdered their way to power in 1978 are not people who are easily stopped." She gave a short, dry laugh. "Israel may have the will to stop them, but the United States holds them in check."

I turned to Sir Leo, making a question with my arched eyebrows.

He gestured to a chair. "Do sit, dear chap." We both sat and he chortled comfortably. "You must forgive Leila. The people of the Middle East tend to be rather intense. The truth is we do retain some friends in Iran and I pop over there from time to time. Leila can't of course, but I act as a sort of mediator for the Labor Party, who maintain fairly cordial relations with most of the Arab world." He sipped. "And at times I mediate for the government, too, on more neutral matters."

I was aware I was being prepped, but wasn't quite sure how to answer. So I decided to make it easy for them.

"I must confess I have never paid much attention to politics. I am aware there is a lot of international pressure on Iran not to make bombs, but than I always figured they would probably use their nuclear energy program as a cover for making weapons-grade plutonium too."

He nodded, "Well, initially, as recently as 2019 in fact, the International Atomic Energy Agency certified that Iran *was* abiding by the international Joint Comprehensive Plan of Action, established in 2015. However, by the summer of that same year, after the United States withdrew from the agreement, the IAEA found that Iran had actually breached the agreement. After that Iran has incurred the wrath of at least half the signatories of the JCPOA because, in November last year, the Atomic Energy Agency found that Iran had been developing centrifuge technology, which is not only explicitly prohibited, but is essential for developing weapons-grade plutonium.

"They also said that Tehran held more than twelve times the amount of enriched uranium permitted under the terms of the JCPOA. There was more, but the gist was that Iran was moving forward with the development of an atomic bomb. Some estimates put Iran at a year or less from having enough weapons-grade plutonium to achieve that aim." He sighed and shook his head. "I'm afraid the White House believes it can induce the Ayatollah back to the negotiating table by threatening to take renewed membership of the Joint Comprehensive Plan of Action off the table. But what the president doesn't understand, what most Western politicians don't understand, is that Iran doesn't give a tinker's toss about the JCPOA. Once they have an atom bomb, they are in the Big Boy's Club, like it or not. And they will be the leaders of the Shi'ite Muslim world."

I gave my head a little twitch and laughed. "That would give the West something to think about."

"Well, to be perfectly honest with you, Dr. Bassett, I find the idea of an Ayatollah with an atom bomb quite alarming, but then, on the other hand, there are two other considerations to be born in mind. The first is that the threat, in reality, is to Israel. Iran has no real beef with Europe, the United Kingdom or America. All they want, really, is the Jews out of Israel. And I mean, you know, frankly..."

He trailed off, watching my face to see my reaction. I smiled and shook my head.

"Like I said, I am not a political animal. I am not anti-Semitic, neither am I anti-Islamic. It just seems to me as long as I can remember the people out there have been shooting each other, and I don't think even they remember why. So I can't really comment." I held his eye a moment and then added, "But you said there were two things to bear in mind. What's the second one?"

"Well—" He smiled and sat back, crossing one leg over the other. "The other is that they are prepared to pay very high prices indeed for anyone who is willing and able to help them. Believe me, the Iranians can be extremely generous when it's in their interest."

"Really? And what kind of help do they look for?" I

turned toward Lady Leila and laughed. "Maybe I could help them out with something. I could use a cash boost!"

They didn't laugh. They smiled, but they didn't laugh, and a silence fell on the room. I looked from one to the other. "Was it something I said?"

It was Sir Leo who answered. "No, no not at all. Well," now he gave a short laugh, "in a sense it is. The fact is, Dr. Bassett, that is part of the reason why I—we—have invited you here."

I made a pretty good show of looking bewildered. "What is?"

"I said we have friends in Iran, in Tehran, who are scientists. Well, the truth is that they are scientists and administrators who are attached to Iran's Atomic Energy Organization, the AEOI. And due to circumstances that need not concern us right now, Iran is actively looking for a team of very specific scientists and engineers. And they are willing to pay top dollar for the right people."

I leaned forward, eyebrows arched high, and gave a small, incredulous laugh. "Are you offering me a job? You invited me to dinner to offer me a job?"

He nodded. "I'm afraid so. I hope you are not offended."

"Offended? No." I sat back again. "A little bewildered... but then top dollar sounds good."

He sighed. "As I am sure you can imagine, after Iran stopped abiding by the Joint Comprehensive Plan of Action, it became difficult, not to say impossible, for her to advertise in the trade journals for top-class professionals in the field. So the government, specifically the AEOI, had to use far more discreet means of advertising its vacancies. And I am one of the people they turn to to make inquiries. As I said, I have a contact in the States who, when I mentioned to him what I was looking for, told me that Dr. Henry Bassett might be looking for work, and was headed to London."

"Wow..." I sipped my drink. "It sounds like I am being drawn into the world of cloaks and daggers. Am I going to be—that is, if I ended up taking the job—would I be at risk? I mean imprisonment, death...?"

He laughed out loud and she laughed with him. It was a convincing performance and you could tell it was not the first time they had done it. It was Leila who answered.

"No, not at all. Outside of the political sphere, Iran functions today much like any other country. As long as you are not some kind of subversive or an agitator, you can just go about your business and the authorities will by and large ignore you. In fact, if you have a prestigious job, such as a rocket engineer, then the chances are you will wield a degree of power through your social status and your contacts."

I lifted my hand. "Wait, wait. This has come a little out of left field. I came here for dinner and suddenly I am seriously considering moving to Iran. We need to slow down a little. I mean, what kind of salary are we talking about? What about accommodation? How long would the contract be for? And then there's the whole issue of what I do when the contract ends. Am I going to be a pariah?"

"My dear fellow, do not distress yourself. There is absolutely no rush for you to make a decision, and it certainly was not my intention to ambush you. Drink up, and let me put your mind at rest. In the first place, as Leila has said, if you toe the line and abide by the rules, Iran is perfectly safe. In fact Sharia law is so severe, Tehran is probably safer than London. Clearly you need some time to think it over and determine how it fits in with your larger life plan, so to speak. But let me give you some facts to help you make an informed decision.

"As to accommodation, you will have a very comfortable apartment on site at the base, and another very comfortable apartment in the best area of Tehran. What will you do afterwards, and will you be a pariah? Quite the opposite is true. In fact we will make it our business to pull strings—and believe me, oil-rich countries like Iran can pull some pretty big strings—and ensure that you move directly from the program into a very respectable university job. As to the duration of the contract and your remuneration..."

He reached in his jacket pocket and pulled out a visiting card. As I took it he said, "This is the fee, in American dollars, for a three-year contract."

On the front, the card had his name, number and address embossed, on the back there was a number. It was the very same number on the sheet of paper Gallin had sent me. As a fee, it was very generous indeed.

"Holy cow..."

"As I say, they can be extremely generous."

The door opened and the butler leaned in. "Dinner is served, sir."

"Oh, splendid." He put his hands on his knees, ready to rise. "Shall we?"

"Yes," I said, deliberately stressing the words as though giving them a double meaning. "Let's!"

FIVE

AT ELEVEN THIRTY THAT NIGHT, AS I WAS toweling myself dry after a shower, the phone rang. It was Gallin's father.

"You are still in London?"

I sat on the bed. "Sure. Why? You have something for me?"

"My daughter's backup. He is willing to talk to you."

"Good, where and when?"

He grunted something that might have been a laugh. "I'm afraid it's not that easy. He is in Tel Aviv. You would have to go there."

"OK. So how do I contact him?" I stood and went to the desk where I sat and switched on my laptop.

"No. He will contact you. You book a room at the Tel Aviv Hilton. He will contact you there. When will you go?"

"I'm booking the ticket now." I paused a couple of minutes while the details appeared on the screen. "I depart at a quarter to eight and arrive at two thirty-five PM. I should be at the hotel by three thirty."

"You will travel as yourself, I presume."

"Not much choice."

"I'll let him know. He'll contact you tomorrow."

I hung up and sat listening to the silence, looking out of the window at the scattered lights of London. The Chief would not like it. It could even cost me my job. But as my grandmother never tired of telling me: you have to do the right thing. I used to ask her, especially when I was older, "How do you know when it's the right thing?" To which she would arch an eyebrow over a penetrating blue eye and say, "You'll know."

And I knew. I could see her wagging a finger at me. "You don't leave a comrade on the field!"

You don't leave a comrade on the field. Even if they're dead.

———

I WASN'T wrong about the Chief. He called at six AM the next morning when I was on my way to the airport in the back of a black cab. He didn't waste any time getting to the point.

"You are booked on a flight to Tel Aviv."

"I knew that."

"I am in no mood for your facetiousness, Alex! I want an explanation!"

"Yes sir. I have a day's grace to give Sir Leo D'Arcy my reply. I don't want to seem overeager, so I am going to Tel

Aviv. I have not checked out of the hotel and I shall be back within thirty-six hours to give Sir Leo my reply."

"There is just one thing I find more infuriating than disobedience, Alex!" I had a moment of synesthesia, where his voice actually sounded puce. "And that is *insolence!*"

"Yes sir."

"Do you suppose me an *imbecile?*"

"No sir, certainly not."

"Then surely you must realize," he said, becoming almost shrill, choking on his own voice, "that I am not asking you what you have done, as clearly I already *know* what you have done! *I am asking you why you are doing it!*"

"Yes, sir."

He took a deep breath while I tried hard to think. Then he asked quietly, "Why are you going to Tel Aviv, Alex?"

"You told me not to tell you things you already knew, sir. And you already know why I am going to Tel Aviv."

"Captain Gallin…" He growled the name. It wasn't a question.

"Yes, sir."

"I specifically told you…"

"I can't do that."

Oddly, that seemed to soften him for a moment. "See reason, Alex. It is an Israeli matter! We cannot interfere in their investigation. Do you seriously believe they are going to let that matter lie? Is there anything you believe you can achieve that the Mossad cannot?"

"They believe she is dead. Even her father thinks she's dead." I couldn't keep the bitterness from my voice. "Fallen in the line of duty."

"You spoke to her father?"

"Yes. How many Israelis fall every year in the line of duty, sir? The kind of man he is, he will not allow them to prioritize her investigation. He is driven by a sense of duty to his country, and I admire that. But it's not good enough for me. If she's dead, I want to know who killed her, and I will make them pay."

His voice started to turn puce again. "Alex, you are acting in *direct* defiance of my orders and I will not tolerate it!"

"Yes, sir."

There was a long, enraged silence. Then, "Well what in the devil's name is that supposed to mean?"

"Sir, I am arriving at the airport and the signal is very bad here. I'll contact you as soon as I get back to the hotel."

I hung up on him, knowing I had probably just flushed my career down the pan. But that was a problem I would have to address later. Right now I had other, much bigger fish to fry.

The flight was long and tedious. Five hours is not quite long enough to have a decent sleep, yet it's too long to kill with a book or a crossword. So I spent most of the time writing down, and studying in detail, everything I knew about the job the Chief had given me, plus Gallin's murder or abduction. And the thing that struck me most forcefully during that process was the fact that it was too much of a coincidence that Gallin and I had both been given the same job.

I had taken only hand baggage and got through customs and passport control pretty quickly. I got a cab and within an hour of landing I was checking in at the front desk of the massive, concrete block which is the Tel Aviv Hilton.

As the concierge handed me my key, he handed me also a sealed envelope. My name was scrawled on it.

I opened it while I was waiting for the elevator. It said simply, *I am probably coming through the doors behind you.*

I folded the note, put it in my breast pocket and the elevator arrived, pinged and the doors slid open. It was a stupid situation and I had no idea what to do next. If I turned around I would be broadcasting that I expected somebody to arrive. So I looked at my watch instead and made to head back toward the reception desk, like I'd forgotten something. That was when I heard the voice from the big glass doors at the entrance.

"Steve?"

It was like déjà vu and I wondered for a moment if it was the only ploy the Mossad ever used. I looked and saw somebody I had never seen before in my life. I frowned and smiled at the same time. I pointed at him and narrowed my eyes. His accent was English middle class with a hint of Transatlantic around his Rs.

"Bob," he said. "Bob Stone. It must be seven or eight years!"

"Sure!" I said, laughing. "I knew the face, but I couldn't place it. Seven years, I'll be damned. How are you?"

"Yeah, yeah. Doing OK. Look at you! You're looking great. Listen, are you busy?"

"Not yet."

"Then drop your bag with the concierge and we'll go get a coffee."

"Sounds good."

I dropped my bag at reception and followed him out to a cream Corolla. We didn't talk until we had climbed in and slammed the doors. Then all he said was, "Don't talk for a bit."

He took me for a long drive, through narrow streets of apartment blocks which mostly had a kind of beige '70s look about them. It struck me that every block was surrounded by trees and gardens, palms and lawns, and though a lot of the apartments were old and rectangular, there was a striking absence of chaos about the place. The Chief was fond of telling me that chaos had become so endemic in our society we didn't even notice it anymore. It was the kind of statement I had learned to nod at and say nothing. But now suddenly I knew what he meant. And suddenly, as we drove through the dappled shade into Ha-Medina Square, Aaron voiced my thoughts.

"We have five borders," he said. "Only two of them are officially, internationally recognized, Jordan and Egypt. Two, Syria and Lebanon, are disputed and then there are the Palestinian territories which are *inside* us. But even then, if that were not enough, the two recognized borders are only as secure as Israel's relationship with the United States. The minute Egypt or Jordan decide they no longer need to worry about the USA, Israel will have five contested borders."

I wasn't sure I was allowed to talk yet so I just looked at him and waited. He turned into Weizmann Street, a broad avenue festooned with palms and plane trees, with the startling skyline dominated by the Marganit Tower and the sprawl of the Tel Aviv hospital.

He gave a small, humorless laugh. "You know it is really bad strategy to fight a war on two fronts. Both Hitler and Napoleon discovered that to their cost in Russia. So you tell me, how wise is it to fight a war on five fronts?"

We turned right past the great, gray concrete slabs of the law courts on Bercovich Street, with their bizarre pyramid, and started to wind a circuitous path among residential streets, apartment blocks and well-ordered gardens.

"We are surrounded on all sides, Mr. Bauer, by people who are not only our enemies, but who want to exterminate us. It is not enough for them to vanquish us, conquer us or subjugate us. No, they will not be satisfied until they wipe us off the face of the planet." He turned to look at me for a second. "This is not something you can deal with logically. There is no negotiating that can go on here. They are uncompromising and out of their minds, out of control." He glanced at me again. "Do you know how dangerous that is? To be crazy and uncompromising *and* out of control at the same time? Their whole existence is predicated on our extermination. That's even worse than Hitler."

He drove in silence for a while, making figures of eight, flicking his eyes at the mirror every five or six seconds.

"We are the only nation on Earth, Mr. Bauer, who live under permanent threat of extinction. With the dedicated agents of our destruction living on our five doorsteps. Many of them enjoying the status of permanent residents inside our country."

Suddenly we pulled out of a side street and we were on the seafront, with the Mediterranean spread out, sparkling in front of us. It was an odd contrast to his apocalyptic speech. He parked, killed the engine and said, "We'll have coffee at the Banana Beach."

"Can I talk yet?"

"We'll get coffee."

We crossed the broad avenue onto the promenade and

then down onto the sand, where we found a beach café with a thatched veranda. We sat. He ordered coffee and I ordered a cold beer. When they were delivered I said:

"You have a reason for telling me all this."

"There are nine and a quarter million people in Israel. Just over six million are Jews, the same number that were exterminated by Hitler, a little less than half of all the Jews in the world. About two million are Arabs, and practically all of those are Sunni Muslims. Beyond our borders there are *three hundred and thirty million* Muslims, and the vast majority of them are radical." He paused. "Can you imagine what would happen—what *could* happen—if those five borders somehow fell? Can you imagine what would happen to Israel, and the Israeli people? Because I can't. It is beyond anything that I can imagine. I just know, in every fiber of my being, that it must never happen." He held my eye for a long moment, then added, "And Aila felt the same way. Her father felt the same way, and every man and woman in the Institute[1] feels the same. Of course it broke the Chief's heart when she was killed. It broke my heart when I realized what had happened, and I was just two minutes away. But it's the price we pay, Mr. Bauer. We have spent millennia fighting for survival, as a nation, but more than a nation, as a family. That conditions the way you see things."

I nodded. "OK, I understand. And I respect everything you are telling me. I do not plan to intrude on anybody's patch or anybody's grief or mourning. I just want to find the bastards who killed her and..." I paused and looked out at the still, glistening sheet of the ocean. Then I looked back at Aaron's thin, intelligent face, with his intense, blue eyes trying to pierce my mind. I gave a small shrug. "Either bring them to justice, or bring justice to them."

"Why? What was Aila to you?"

I surprised myself by hesitating for a moment. "We connected. It was private between me and her. It doesn't concern anybody else. She had my back. I had hers. So I owe her."

He sighed and looked away, observing absently the people coming in and out of the café, noting where they sat and what they did. He never stopped, I realized. He probably slept with his eyes open.

"You were lovers?"

"That's none of your goddamn business, but no, we weren't."

"There is probably not much I can tell you. What do you want to know?"

"I want to know what happened that day. I know why she was there. She was applying for a job in Tehran. Let's leave it at that. I want to know every detail of what went down. You know the drill. Anything at all that might be helpful in giving me Ahmed's identity, and where I can find him."

He snorted. "Is that all? You think if I had that kind of information we wouldn't already have the bastard?"

I felt a slow hot burn in my gut. "I don't know, Aaron. I don't know what your policies or priorities are. But I do know one thing. If I was in your shoes, I'd be grateful of every bit of help I could get, and I wouldn't be doing everything in my power to reject it." I leaned forward. "I am trying to help."

"Thanks, but we don't need your help."

"All right. I am not trying to help. I am trying to find the man, or men, who killed my friend. Are *you* willing to help *me?* I might mention, while I am at it, that I have the old man's blessing." I pointed at him. "You know that because he told you to come talk to me."

"I told you, I'll do what I can."

"Good, so how about you quit the smart commentary and tell me what you know. I want to know what *you* would want to know if you were sitting in my place."

He took a deep breath and blew, looking at the sea. Then he shrugged and I could see there were tears in his eyes.

"It's hard. It was Friday. I had got my instructions the night before. I wasn't party to the whole briefing. We don't operate that way. Everything is need to know. The only people who knew everything were Aila and Ariel, her father, Mr. Gallin, the Chief. I had to drive to Campden Hill Road and wait. I had to be there by five thirty PM. She would drive past at just after six. I had her license plate and the make and color of the car. When she passed I was to follow her at a discreet distance, and stay in contact. She had a nano earpiece and a mic. At six o'clock she drove past. I checked my mirror, nobody was following, so I pulled out after her."

"Then what happened?"

"Then," he sighed again, "then things started to go wrong."

SIX

MEANWHILE, NINE HUNDRED AND SIXTY-FIVE MILES away, in a small town on the southern shore of the Caspian Sea, a thug in a uniform pushed open a door to a seedy office and Gallin was hurled, naked and shivering, to the tiled floor.

She looked up and saw an old wooden desk. Beneath it a cable fed an ancient fan heater with electricity. Just beyond the heater she saw two leather boots. She raised herself up and saw beyond the desk a window with a view of gray skies and a red-roofed building. And between the window and the desk a man in a colonel's uniform, watching her with distaste. He gestured at her and spoke to the guards who had dragged her in. She heard one of them depart.

He looked back at her and shook his head. "You must be cold. It gets cold in this part of Iran in the autumn. You should not be sitting on the floor with no clothes on."

His face said he was sincere, but she knew he was taunting her. He gave the ghost of a smile and stroked his pencil moustache. "The police, you know? They are the most brutish people in our society. If you want to take the police examination in Iran, they ask you two questions. First, how much is two and two? If you answer four, you are too smart for the police. The second question is, if ordered to shoot your mother, what would you say? The correct answer is, 'I would not speak, I would shoot.'"

Behind her one of the cops came in, put a bentwood chair beside her and draped a rough blanket around her shoulders. The colonel gestured at the chair.

"Please, sit."

She pulled the blanket around her, got to her feet and sat in the chair.

"Why are you doing this to me? I was offered a job..."

"Please, let us not waste time. I do not want to hurt you. I am happy to negotiate your release and return to Israel, or London, wherever you prefer. All I ask in return is information. You are an Israeli spy."

She began to weep. "For God's sake! I am not an Israeli spy! I don't know where you got this idea from! I wouldn't know how to *begin* to be a spy! I'm a scientist, and a damn good one. I just want a job. I don't know why you are doing this. What have I done?"

"You met with our representative in London?"

"Yes! You know I did."

"Whom did you meet?"

"He just said his name was Ahmed."

"Ahmed? Describe him."

"Tall, strong, short hair, clean-shaven, brown eyes, leather jacket..."

"You are very observant."

"Yeah, I'm a scientist. It's what we do."

"And what did you discuss?"

She closed her eyes and took a deep breath.

"He said I was late. I gave him some wise-ass answer and he said I didn't talk like a rocket engineer. I thought it was a stupid thing to say and I gave him some grief about it. He told me he had to be careful. Then he said I was Jewish, like he didn't know that already. I got mad. I get reminded every day by my parents, by people who aren't Jewish and now by you. All I want is to not be *anything*. I just want to do my job and be a person!"

She took a deep breath. He didn't say anything. She closed her eyes again and went on.

"I told him yes, I was Jewish, so what? And then the son of a bitch wanted to know how I could betray my people. Basically I told him I had no interest in politics, in the power games played by the United States and Israel, and that I do not identify as a Jew. I am English, whatever that means, and my grandparents were a Jew and a Palestinian. So then he said I was a Muslim. And I told him I wasn't a Jew, a Muslim or a Christian. I'm not even an atheist. I told him all I was interested in was working and making money. He told me I disgusted him. I got mad and we didn't make friends."

She sighed and opened her eyes. "OK," she said. "If that is what this is all about I am willing to apologize. I am sorry if I was offensive..."

He raised both hands and shook his head. "That is not necessary. Please, continue with what you were telling me. I will arrange for a better cell, and for them to return your clothes."

She closed her eyes again, recalling the meeting in the

pub. "I asked him what the salary was. He wrote it down on a piece of paper and told me it was in US dollars for three years' work and would be paid at the end of the job. It was a very generous salary, but I don't work for free and I told him I would need half upfront. He said he'd have to check with his superiors. He also said that when the job was done you would fix me up with a job in an American university. We wrangled some more. He said he'd be in touch and that was it."

"No." He shook his head again. "There is more. You asked for something."

Gallin's jaw dropped. "Is that what this is all about? I don't believe it. I asked for fifty quid to cover my expenses that night. You are mad about *that?*"

He laughed. "No, not at all. Receive that with our blessings. But where are the note and the money now?"

She frowned, like she was giving it thought.

"Um, in my purse, I guess. Or in my car."

"Not in your purse, we have checked. Where is your car?"

"At my house."

"You arrived in a taxi. Where did you leave your car, Captain Gallin?"

She stared at him, and felt the cold spider legs of terror crawl over her skin.

———

FAR ABOVE THE Pacific Ocean Sarah snored softly and Aunt Peg looked down at the vast blue-blackness of the sea, where the sun's light lay shattered, shining a path that led nowhere. She felt again the warm twist of anxiety in her gut. It was a feeling she was not accustomed to. Her father had always ensured that their family never had anything to feel anxious about. He had been a true patriarch, a good Christian and loving (if strict!) father. He didn't drink, he didn't gamble, and was never to be found at the bar. He was a family man, a rock.

So none of them had ever felt that empty pit of anxiety that she felt now so acutely; the feeling that things were spiraling out of control. She made a silent prayer asking for the Lord's guidance. Sarah was swimming out into deep, dark water, and Aunt Peg felt desperately out of her depth.

She turned and looked at Sarah sleeping beside her, and for a moment felt a flash of anger at the child's naïve selfishness. Who was this Ali? What did she know about him? And all his damned cousins! Suleiman and Hussein and Mustafa and this damned Raza! And now they had to go to the Bronx to deliver...

Her thoughts seemed to trail off as she looked down at the vast ocean again, with the sheet of glaring light hiding its darkness.... To deliver an amulet; an amulet given to his great, great-grandfather by the imam Ali ibn whatever, and passed down, from generation to generation, until it reached cousin Suleiman, who now wanted it given to his son Raza.

Inscribed with the words of the prophet.

Another rush of anger. *The* prophet? He wasn't *her* prophet. She was an American and a good Christian! She felt a sudden, violent need to reject Ali and all the menacing strangeness he—*and* Sarah—had brought, unbidden, into her life. And as she thought that, the amulet thrust itself into her mind again.

An amulet?

She thought back to the box, elaborately wrapped in gift paper. It had struck her when they handed it over that it was too big to be a simple amulet. Ali had explained that it was contained in a beautiful rosewood box, but it still hadn't convinced her. And not only that, he had told Sarah, while kissing and caressing her, that if they asked any questions at customs, to say simply it was a gift for a friend, and that she had packed it herself.

Aunt Peg crossed her arms and set her jaw. She and Sarah had *not* packed it themselves and they did *not* know what was in the parcel. She, for one, would be very glad when this whole thing was over.

But even as she said it she had a strange sense of foreboding, and she wondered if it would ever be over.

SEVEN

"Go wrong how?" I asked.

"You probably know," he sat forward and put his elbows on the table, then offered me a rueful smile, almost like a token of peace, "that Aila can be pretty reckless. When she gets an idea in her head, she just goes for it." He wasn't really looking for an answer so I didn't give him one. He shook his head, smiling, remembering. "We were all pretty hyped. I don't think there's an Israeli in the country—or a Jew in the world! —who hasn't been expecting to hear, sooner or later, that Iran has an atom bomb. But one thing is a hypothetical expectation, however well-founded, and something very different is receiving official confirmation. We were all pumped, tense, needing to act fast. But," he laughed, "that just meant that the rest of us were now the way Aila is all the time. So you can imagine what Aila was like. She was on the next level."

His face drained of all expression. His eyes became abstracted. "So I pulled out behind her, and she was off.

Fifty miles per hour toward the Kensington Town Hall. If I had kept up with her it would have looked like a car chase through sleepy Kensington. The police would have been on us in a couple of minutes."

Gallin was intense by anybody's standards, but I was having trouble buying Gallin as irresponsible or unprofessional. I decided to keep the fact to myself in favor of keeping the flow going. "You said you had radio contact with each other."

He nodded. "Yeah, and as soon as she took off I called her: 'Hey, what are you doing? You in a race with somebody? Slow down, yadda yadda.'" He spread his hands and shrugged, smiling ruefully again. "You can imagine the answer. This is Aila, right? 'What's the matter with you, Aaron? You left your balls at home? Didn't they teach you how to drive?'"

I heard some children shout, the splash of water. A warm breeze flapped the parasols on the sand.

"So what happened?"

"I knew the route she was going to take. So I followed that route, and made sure I had a brief exchange with her every minute or so, so I knew she was OK. You know, stuff like, 'Hey, slow down, will you.' To which she would reply 'Sure thing. Mummy,' but at least I knew she was OK."

"OK, so she got there well ahead of you."

"She parked on Old Queen Street and walked round the corner to the pub—"

"What pub?"

"The Westminster Arms, on Storey's Gate. That would be about six thirty. By the time I arrived, about ten minutes later, maybe a little more, she was already inside talking to this guy."

"So nobody went in the pub with her?"

"No, the plan was I would go in about two minutes after her. She would give me a sign when she was finishing up and I would leave before her and tail her home. But by the time I got there and parked on Storey's Gate, she was already negotiating the salary and preparing to leave. I figured I had best wait for her in the car. And it's a good job I did, because she came out just about the time I would have been ordering a drink.

"Then she does another one of her brilliant stunts. Instead of driving out where I was, so I could follow her, she reverses at high speed down Old Queen Street and leaves via Parliament Square and Whitehall." He shrugged. "Again, there was no way I could catch up with her. I followed the agreed route and eventually tried to contact her. There was no reply, so I called the Chief. I guess you know the rest."

I ran it through in my head while I stared at the beer on the table in front of me. I realized I hadn't touched it.

"How did you go about connecting with Ahmed?"

He shook his head. "I have no idea. Like I said, we are all in cells and nobody know what goes on in the other cells. We put the word out that this unemployed scientist was available. She was brilliant but her career is on the rocks because she has a bad attitude. That kind of thing. And after a while Ahmed contacted her, asked if she wanted to meet."

"You weren't involved in that process?"

"No."

"Do you know who was?"

"Of course not. You would have to ask Ariel, but he won't tell you."

"That's not a whole lot of help."

"I'm sorry. It's the best I can do. We tend to deal with things in house."

"Yeah." I sighed. "I know. Well, if it's any help, I am working unofficially and without the blessing of my department. In fact by tomorrow I may not have a job." I tossed him my card. "If you think of anything, or decide I might be helpful, I'll probably take a stroll up to the Little Prague Restaurant, on Ben Yehuda Street. About eight."

"Yeah?" He looked out at the sea and seemed to think for a moment. Then he shrugged. "OK, I'll give it some thought. Maybe I'll join you for a glass of wine." He hesitated. "I have not been very hospitable. This is a delicate subject on many levels. But let me say that I do appreciate what you are doing. Just," he shrugged again, "don't get in the way."

"Got it."

I stood and we shook, and I walked the mile and a bit along the seafront back to my hotel trying to make sense of the conversation I'd just had. I hadn't really learnt anything significant that I didn't know already, but there was something about his account that was nagging at me. It made me smile. The thumbnail sketch he'd drawn of Gallin was something I was familiar with, and his admiration for her shone through the frustration and the pain he obviously felt. He had made her out to be almost incompetently irresponsible, though, and I wondered if that was wounded, male pride or something else.

I stopped at the Spiegel Park to look out at the sea, like

molten silver melted by the sun, and suddenly, as I thought it through, Gallin's reckless behavior did not seem so amusing after all. I turned away from the ocean and pulled my cell from my pocket. I dialed in the code for ODIN as I picked my way through the scrub and the ancient ruins, back toward the path toward the hotel.

Lovelock put me through voice recognition and I snarled at her, "I need to talk to the Chief, now."

"He said to tell you he will not talk to you until you return to London."

"Tell him I'm in London! Tell him whatever you need to tell him! Put me through now!"

"I can see you're in Tel Aviv, Alex."

"*Now!*"

There was thirty seconds of silence, then the Chief's voice, petulant, "What? I don't want to speak to you! You are disobedient! Insubordinate!"

"I know what happened to Captain Aila Gallin."

He faltered, then, "So what? I have told you, Alex, that is not our case and you must leave it to the Israelis! I *will not tolerate* insubordination!"

"Sir, you don't understand..."

"*I understand perfectly!* I told you not to investigate her death and you have *directly* disobeyed my orders! You have spoken to the head of the Mossad's field office in London, you have traveled to Tel Aviv... *My god, man!*"

"Sir, I apologize, but you have to let me explain what I have..."

"*Shut up! Before you give me a stroke!* You will return directly to London and you will finish your mission, or you will face the most severe disciplinary action! *Do you under-*

stand? And you will leave the investigation of Captain Gallin's death to the Israelis!"

I bit hard on my teeth and snarled, "Yes, sir!"

I didn't go directly to London. I made a detour via the Hilton's bar and had a large Macallan, no ice. Then I went to my room to pack and bring my flight back to London forward to that evening. But when I opened my laptop and looked at the screen, I thought about what Aaron had said when I'd given him my card and told him I was going to have dinner at the Little Prague Restaurant, on Ben Yehuda Street, if he thought of anything else.

He'd become thoughtful, looking out at the sea, like something was on his mind. What had he said? "...I'll give it some thought." I rolled the words around in my brain like a fine whisky. "I'll give it some thought." What was "it"? What exactly was he going to give some thought to, if he'd already told me everything he knew? Then he'd added, "Maybe I'll join you for a glass of wine," and he'd apologized for his lack of hospitality. Was he building bridges? Trying to make peace? Distancing himself, as Gallin's friend, from the official position?

I closed the airline's booking page and shut down the computer. Nero could go burn Rome. I was going to talk to Aaron. I had questions I needed answered.

I LEFT the hotel on foot at about half past seven. It was a pleasant evening, and I figured it would take me half an hour to stroll to the restaurant, through the Independence Park gardens, down the broad, busy sweep of HaYarkon Street and then east along Arlozorov Street, among the pines, the palms and the plane trees that occupied every inch of free space. Until I came to the warm, evening bustle of Ben Yehuda, with cafés, grocery stores and restaurants spilling out onto the sidewalks among the growing dusk, where lights and headlamps were beginning to wink on, where the evening air was beginning to carry the rich smells of Mediterranean food and thoughts were turning to cold beer, hot food, and wine.

I sat at a table out on the pavement and ordered a pilsner. The waitress brought it to me with the menu and a small dish of olives. I had drained my beer and was just telling the waitress I wanted a seafood salad and a baked goose leg served with baked apples and a garnish of my choice, when a husky voice that had smoked too much and was now trying to be good, said, "Henry?"

The waitress went away and I looked up to see a woman in a scarlet coat, with black hair and black eyes and legs that should have had a content warning on them. It was one of those saxophone moments. For a second I even wished I'd had a Camel, so I could have squinted at her through the smoke and called her sugar. Instead I said, "Of all the gin joints in all the towns in all the world, you had to walk into mine."

She laughed. "Oh, Henry! Don't you recognize me?"

"Sure I do. You were in my dreams last night. I almost didn't wake up. Your legs are even better in real life."

She tilted her head on one side and raised an eyebrow. "Funny. Mind if I sit down?"

"I'd mind if you didn't. Did you come to tell me Aaron can't make it?" I stood and held the chair for her while she sat. "What will you drink?"

"A Tubi Sixty."

I told the waitress and then turned to my old friend whom I did not recognize. I said, facetiously, "Hawaii, 2018? The Riviera last fall? Venice that November." I shook my head. "The face haunts me, yet I can't put a place or a name to it." She didn't laugh. She kept a fixed smile on her face.

"She said you were funny."

"She did, did she? She's pretty funny herself."

"Was."

I gave a small twitch to my head. "*That's* not funny. Are you going to tell me your name or shall I invent one?"

"My name is Marion. We met in New York. I'm not sure if you live there, or what you were doing there. It was at an art exhibition. Coming back to you?"

I snapped my fingers. "Damien Hirst, but we only saw half the exhibit."

"We got drunk and went back to your hotel, promising not to share any details about each other."

"How very *Last Tango* of us. Are we going to do that again tonight? Last rumba in Tel Aviv?"

"Why not?"

"Do you mind if I eat my goose leg first? Assuming the goose had two legs, there is probably a spare one going for you."

The smile was fading from her face. "You don't seem to be taking this very seriously."

"See? You don't know me the way she did. She knew that when I was facetious, I was at my most deadly serious. Stay till the pudding. That way we won't attract attention."

The waitress delivered the seafood salad and I asked for a plate for Marion.

"Share with me," I said, "and pretend to be enjoying yourself."

She leaned forward and stabbed the salad with a fork, like she was trying to kill it.

"Aaron is waiting," she said under her breath.

"Let him wait. He shouldn't send beautiful women to do his dirty work for him."

She sighed and stuffed salad in her mouth, chewed watching me. "You really liked her, didn't you."

I spoke around a mouthful of prawns and avocado. "I'm getting a little tired of this past tense all the time. Have you seen the body?"

"No."

"Do you know anyone who has?"

She shook her head. "But live here long enough and you get in the habit of not building up false hope."

"How do you square that with never giving up hope?"

"You never pin your hopes on one single person, and you get used to the idea that people you love are going to die, keeping your hope alive. And one day it will probably be your turn. And when that day comes, then you know that the people who love you will mourn you, and let you go."

I was quiet, then nodded. "OK, I apologize. But I am not there yet."

"How could you be? You are surrounded by the Pacific, the Atlantic, Canada, and Mexico in the south. We live in Pearl Harbor every day."

"I get it. But I need to find her, or at least know what happened to her."

"It's personal."

I nodded. "Yeah, it's pretty personal."

"Ok, so finish your salad and your goose, and let's go."

I took my time finishing the salad. She sighed a couple of times but sipped her drink and tried to appear patient.

"You seem nervous," I said eventually, as I cut into the goose.

"I don't like wasting time."

"Is that what we're doing? Wasting time?" She didn't answer, just watched me. "I'll tell you what," I said, laughing like she'd said something funny. "If I were an Iranian operative, or Hezbollah, sitting across the road right now, watching you, I'd think there was something wrong. So I'll tell you what I am going to do. I am going to sit here and eat, and drink and laugh, until you relax. And when you start laughing and drinking and acting natural, then we'll leave and make like we're going back to my hotel." I laughed again and leaned forward. "Because, I'll tell you what, Marion. Your lack of professionalism is making me very nervous."

She stared at me a moment like she wanted to eat my liver. Then she threw back her head and laughed, sipped her drink and put her hand on my knee.

"Fine," she said, like she was describing the negligee she'd just bought. "But finish your damn meal and let's get the hell out of here."

EIGHT

She had a Range Rover waiting down the road. She climbed in behind the wheel and I got in beside her. The streetlamps washed the lower part of her face with orange light, but her eyes remained in shadow. I saw her lips smile. She pressed the starter and the big engine hummed into life.

She asked, "You OK?"

It was a stupid question so I didn't answer. Instead I said, "Where are we going?"

"To see Aaron." She pulled out and we moved south along Ben Yehuda, then took a right down toward the beach.

"That's what for," I said. "I'm asking you where."

"You wouldn't know it if I told you. You'll see when we get there."

I watched in silence as we moved among slightly dilapidated, boxy apartment blocks, four and five stories high. A central, pedestrianized walkway said this had once aspired to be an elegant, middle-class area. Now, the walls that had once been painted an elegant ochre, understated cream and ill-advised blue, were peeling to reveal the ugly concrete beneath.

The walkway, eerie in the dappled light that shone through the trees, rose to a pedestrian bridge that led to Atarim Square. We turned right and followed the road around, to pass under the square. We emerged onto the seafront, with the beach on our right. There was no moon and little traffic, and we cruised along past the tall palms, silhouetted against the deep turquoise sky, and the straight, functional '70s apartment blocks on our left, which now, oddly, spoke of a saner age.

The streetlamps washed past in a steady pulse. I looked at Marion's face. She was beautiful, but her expressionlessness robbed her of that beauty and made her almost mechanical. We wound gently along the coast, with the bars and restaurants sliding by on our left, and a strange certainty began to settle on me.

We passed Banana Beach in silence and then bore right toward Old Jaffa. Here the rectangular concrete blocks of downtown were replaced by ancient sandstone buildings two or three stories high, with arches and awnings among narrow, twisting streets. This was suddenly the southern Mediterranean of Bogart, *Casablanca* and *Indiana Jones*. The narrow streets teemed with milling humanity, tourists talking, drinking, eating, kidding themselves they were exploring a different culture, when all they were really doing was spreading their own on the tides of market forces.

For a while I thought maybe this was where we were

going, to one of these dark backstreets, but we kept moving. We crossed Yossi Carmel Square and turned out along the Jaffa Port Road. After that there was more twisting and turning down narrow roads among tumble-down, dilapidated buildings that might have been anything from two hundred to two thousand years old or more. Many of the streets had no lighting, and were little more than the spaces between houses. We threaded our way through the maze and I soon lost track of where we were. I figured somewhere in the Bat Yam district, near the sea, but that was about as good as it got.

And then suddenly we were out of the old town, onto a broad, brightly lit avenue which we followed into the broad, ill-lit desolation of an industrial sector. Steel roller blinds slipped by in a procession of the dead, among pools of wan light that revealed nothing, but cast secret shadows behind crumbling walls and into secret corners.

A couple more turns and we were on the beach again, and I realized we were now outside the city. I could see tall tower blocks off to the left, beyond the dark hulks of low hills. There were palm trees here and there, and large expanses of wasteland.

She slowed, turned to the right, killed the lights and we rocked and bobbed over an expanse of barren, pitted earth until we came to an anonymous Honda that was parked in the shadow of a small beach bar which stood silent and dark against the sea. Here she killed the engine and said, "You wanted to know where we were going. Well, this is it."

"There was a finality about the way she said it."

"You're going to kill me."

"You know what happened to the cat."

"Curiosity killed it."

She nodded and outside a car door slammed. I looked and saw that two men had climbed out of the Toyota and were approaching the Range Rover. When I looked back at her she had a Glock 17 in her hand and was pointing it at me. I shook my head, just once.

"Why?"

"See? There you go again."

The door opened and Aaron and some other guy with a big beard were pointing suppressed semiautomatics at me. Aaron said, "Get out and take it real easy."

I stepped down from the truck and stood with my hands raised to the height of my head, and repeated my question. "Why, Aaron? I can't believe you've sold out to Iran or Hezbollah."

"I guess you'll never know, Mason. And you know what? There is no reason why you should. This is not your fight. I told you to butt out, but you wouldn't listen. Now," he gestured with his gun toward the beach bar, "over there."

I smiled but didn't move. "I have three people pointing guns at me, probably with the intention of killing me, and you tell me this is not my fight?"

"Don't make this harder than it is, Mason."

"Harder?" I laughed. "Seriously? Who for, you or me?"

Marion didn't let him answer. "C'mon, Aaron! What does it matter where we do it? Here, by the beach bar, wherever! We can't spend all night here! Just do it already!"

"Shut up, Marion!"

"Yeah, shut up, Marion," I agreed. "You don't want the

body found till as late as possible tomorrow. Am I right, Aaron?"

"Shut up, Mason. Now move, I don't want to hurt you. We'll make this painless."

Marion shoved me with surprising force and I took a few steps toward the beach bar.

"So what's this about? You killed Gallin?"

I obviously touched a nerve because Aaron spun on me and thrust his suppressed Sig in my face. "I did *not* kill Aila!"

His bearded friend muttered, "Take it easy. Stay cool."

And Marion said, "Shut up, Aaron!"

I said, "What is this, a shut-up fest?" and a sharp pain bit into my back below my shoulder blade. "You too, Mason. Just shut up!"

I swore softly and kept walking slowly, trying to ignore the pain that was making it hard to breathe.

"So if you didn't kill her, why the coverup?"

This time she brought the butt of her Glock down hard on my shoulder and she kicked me in the back of the knee. Fortunately I was expecting it and managed to dodge the worst of the blow on my shoulder. But the kick in the knee was agony. She kicked me again in the thigh and spoke through gritted teeth.

"*I told you to shut the fuck up!*"

Aaron snarled, "All right! That's enough! He's an ally! We treat him with respect!"

I got up on one knee and looked back at where Marion had stepped up to Aaron and had thrust her lovely face into his and was stabbing his chest with her finger. "Ally? *Ally?* If they were our damned allies we wouldn't be in this situation in the first place! We are facing a damned extinction event, pal! Because of your damned friends and allies! Now do what you gotta do or I will!"

I got painfully to my feet, exaggerating the damage she had done to my leg. I didn't have to try all that hard. I raised my hands and limped toward them. I spoke directly to Aaron.

"You do not want to do this. We had one administration that let you down, but the US is your ally and if you go through with this you could jeopardize that support. Not so much because you killed one of her agents, but because they'll want to know why." I pointed at him. "If I go back to DC and tell this story, they will choose not to believe me. I am going to get fired anyhow. I was ordered not to come here and I was told this is your affair, not ours. Let me go and there will be no consequences. But kill me, and ODIN will come after you, so will Ariel Gallin, and so will your own government. Israel cannot afford to attack the US." I wagged the finger I was using to point at him. "And you need to remember, ODIN knows I am here." I grinned. "That is *why* they are going to fire me. If I don't go back, they *will* be asking why."

Marion said something vile and thumped Aaron on the chest. "They find his body on the beach, his wallet missing, he was last seen leaving a bar with a sexy woman...nothing connects him to us."

I butted in. "You seriously think, having been ordered by my boss to return to London tonight, they will buy the theory that I didn't go because I went to meet a hooker? Are you out of your minds? What the hell have you got yourselves into? Pal," I addressed Aaron again, "you are getting seriously out of your depth, and you keep listening to this crazy woman and you are going to wind up in a world of trouble. You want to stop this before you completely lose control."

For a moment I thought I had him. I saw him hesitate and his eyes falter. And for just an instant I saw frustration replace resolve on Marion's face. She felt she was losing him, and the whole situation was about to shift. And that was when the bearded guy intervened, solid, calm and unwavering.

"It's too late for that, Aaron. We have to finish what we started. We kill him, we sanitize the scene and we go."

It was training, procedure, protocol: things they all understood. Aaron looked me in the eye and I knew he was going to do it. He said, "Sorry," and he and the beard stepped in to grab my arms. Marion was right behind them.

I hated doing what I did. It is an almost religious tenet with me that a man must never hit a woman. But the situation was out of hand and, as my grandmother used to say, needs must when the devil drives. So I seized the moment. The guys were moving in to grab my arms, which meant their weapons were not pointed at me, and she was closing in, which meant if she shot me she'd risk shooting her pals too. It was now or never.

I grabbed their collars, one in each fist, used them as support and lashed out with the leg she had so recently bruised. My instep connected in a low kick between her lovely legs and I saw the expression of astonished agony crumple her face in slow motion. As my foot touched the ground I let go of their collars and hunkered down. Aaron's fist swung over my head and my right fist plunged into his lower belly. I felt the beard's leg pressing against me and in a reflex that took less than half a second my elbow crashed back into his knee. He fell and I was on my feet. I stamped hard where no one should ever stamp hard, knelt on his solar plexus and smashed a straight right into the tip of his jaw.

"If you'd kept your mouth shut," I told him, "you might have walked away from this with your tackle intact."

Aaron and Marion were semiconscious, so I gagged them with socks and tied their wrists and ankles with bootlaces, then ejected their magazines and dumped the weapons and the magazines into the trunk of the Honda, the keys to which I helpfully tossed into the sand in the shadow of a palm tree.

Finally I patted Aaron awake and spoke quietly into his face.

"This time you got away with your life, because we are allies and I don't know what kind of stupid game you got pulled into. But do this to me again and I will kill you. All three of you. Think it over, Aaron. I don't know you, but I think you're better than this."

He didn't answer. He couldn't. He had a sock in his mouth.

I took the keys to the Range Rover from Marion and drove the truck back into town. I turned the incident over in my head as I crawled through the winding streets of the old city. The ancient sandstone walls, painted amber by old, iron lamps, cast deep shadows in archways and alleyways, like the dark shadows in my mind where I didn't want to go. I decided it all confirmed the hypothesis I had wanted to explain to Nero.

All I wanted to know was whether Gallin was alive. If she was alive, I wanted to know where she was so I could go get her. If she was dead, I wanted to know who had killed her, so I could go and get them. But the more I looked and the more I learned, the more complicated the picture became; and the more I was forced to look into those deep shadows where a truth lay, a truth as ancient as Israel and the Jews, a truth I did not want to see.

I dumped the Range Rover on Dizengoff Street and pushed into the first bar I found. It was crowded and noisy. I ordered a double Macallan straight up and took it into a corner where I sat at a small table and called Ariel Gallin.

"I told you not to contact me."

"Unless Aila was alive. I think she is." He didn't say anything, but I could hear him suppressing sobs on the other end of the line. I said, "But I need you to explain something to me. I was just kidnapped by three Katsas. One of them was Aaron. They took me down to the beach and they were going to kill me. Did you order them to do that?"

"Of course not."

"In that case we have a big problem."

I didn't need to explain it to him. He had seen it as soon as I had asked him the question. What he said shouldn't have taken me by surprise, but it did.

"Are you a religious man, Alex?"

"No."

"For us, everything is religion. Religion is everything. And this tree, the Judeo-Christian tree, with its three great branches, is a troubled religion with a vengeful, warlike god." He sighed heavily. "Damascus," he said, "is the oldest continually inhabited city on the planet. Did you know that? But Isaiah 17 tells us, 'See, Damascus will no longer be a city, but will become a heap of ruins. The cities of Aroer will be deserted, left to flocks which will lie down with no one to make them afraid. The fortified city will disappear from Ephraim, and royal power from Damascus, the remnant of Aram will be the glory of the Israelites, declares the Lord God.'"

I scowled. "What are you talking about, Ariel?"

He ignored me and went on, "On that day their strong cities, which they left because of the Israelites, will be like places abandoned to thickets and undergrowth, and all will be desolation."

"Ariel, you are not making sense. Talk to me, what is this about?"

"'What is it about? It is about God, Allah, Yahweh, Elohim...and which name of God is the true name of God, and who are the children of the true God. It is about the House of Israel and Ezekiel 38 and 39."

He intoned again, "Gog shall come with his armies, with Persia, Ethiopia and Libya, all of them with shield and helmet—Gomer and all his bands, the house of Togarmah and all his bands. Be thou prepared,' he tells Gog and his allies, 'and prepare for thyself, thou and all thy company that are assembled unto thee, and be thou a guard unto them. For I shall turn thee back and leave but a sixth part of thee, and I will cause thee to come up from the north and I will bring thee upon the mountains of Israel, and I will smite the bow from thy left hand and I will cause thine arrows to fall from thy right hand. Thou shall fall upon the mountains of Israel, thou and all thy bands, and the people who are with thee. I will give thee unto the ravenous birds and the beasts to be devoured. Thou shalt fall upon the field, for I have spoken it, sayeth the Lord God."

"Ariel, will you cut it out! What are you talking about?"

"I am talking about Russia, Iran and the nation of Islam marching on Israel, and about how Israel, according to prophecy, will annihilate her enemies, rendering Damascus nothing but a ruin. I am talking about the end of days."

I didn't ask anymore. I hung up and drank deep.

NINE

I didn't hang around after that. I collected my stuff from the hotel, chartered an air taxi to Athens and, as dawn was leaking into the eastern Mediterranean horizon, I boarded a flight to London Gatwick and slept all the way.

I arrived at the Dorchester just before midday, ducked through the rain into the lobby, went up to my room, ordered a large pot of black coffee and a full, English breakfast, and then stood groaning under the shower for fifteen minutes.

When room service knocked, I was in a bathrobe, toweling my hair. I opened the door and found the waiter pushing a trolley and looking embarrassed because he had a man in a suit behind him, sporting a tired face.

"Your coffee and croissants, sir."

I stood aside to let him in and offered a chilly smile to the man in the suit. He said, "Are you Alex Mason?"

"Why do you ask?"

"Because if you are, I need to talk to you." He offered me

a smile almost as chilly as my own and added, "My name is Walter D. Hall. It was my daughter's birthday. She's five. We were watching *Beauty and the Beast*, and we were about to bring out the cake, pretend the lights had gone, candles, you know the drill."

"That's rough."

"No, that's lovely. What's rough is the Chief calling up and saying, 'I need you to go to London this very instant."

"You told him about the cake?"

"He asked if it was shop bought. Can I come in? I've been sitting in the lobby all night."

I told the boy to bring more coffee and more croissants. When he'd gone we sat at the table and ate in silence for a moment. When he'd finished the first croissant and his first cup, he said, "I'm supposed to get tough on you."

"Oh. What about?"

"C'mon, you know what about. You have to go to Iran, and forget the private investigation you're conducting. The Mossad will take care of that."

I frowned. "You know the details?"

"No, of course not. I'm just passing on a message. Chief says you need to confirm the offer today and ship out to Tehran, or you will spend the rest of your miserable life eating processed, packaged food on a tray in front of the TV, and cooking in a microwave." He spread his hands and shrugged. "I memorized that bit. He also said you would be suspended without pay and he would personally ensure you never worked again, anywhere. I should tell you that when he said that, his eyes were kind of wild, his hair was all kind of standing up, and he had spittle on his lips. Have you ever seen him like that?"

"Couple of times. They say he was like that when he burned down the restaurant in Paris."

"Yeah, I heard that story. I think you should go to Iran. This other thing, let the Mossad deal with it."

I called Lovelock, confirmed that Nero had had a hissing fit and had sent Walter to threaten me with a lifetime of TV dinners, and told her to tell the Chief I was back in London and about to accept the job.

"Oh, baby," she crooned, "and I was so looking forward to the funeral."

I left Walter fully dressed in his coat, sleeping on the bed, and made my way out to the street. The rain had settled in, there were creeping chills making their way up trouser legs and down shirt collars, and beside the entrance to the hotel a gutter was splashing water onto the sidewalk. I went and stood beside it and called Sir Leo D'Arcy.

"This is Sir Leo D'Arcy's residence."

"Good morning, this is Dr. Henry Bassett..."

"Ah, yes, Dr. Bassett. Sir Leo has been expecting your call. He will be very pleased to hear from you. Please hold the line."

A few seconds later D'Arcy came on. "Dr. Bassett. How are you? I hope our weather isn't getting you down too much. Have you had a think?"

"I have."

"And...?"

"I am delighted to accept your offer."

He actually laughed. "Ah! Splendid! Splendid! I am delighted."

"So, what happens now?"

GALLIN STARED at the man across the desk. Her lower lip curled and trembled, tears spilled from her eyes, she shook her head. In her mind she assessed his height at five-ten, about the same as her. He was scrawny for a man, not big in the chest, arms or shoulders.

"Please," she said, "what do I need to do to convince you? There has been some mistake somewhere. I am a scientist! You've seen my resumé! You can check my references! Call the university." She stared into his eyes and saw the complacent greed for power, the lust for subjugation, and let the blanket slip over her shoulder, allowing him to see just enough. "Just tell me what I have to do," she repeated, "what you want from me. I'll do it. Anything. All I want is to get to work. Please, help me..."

His eyes prowled over her body, lingering on the suggested curves, then locked onto her own weeping, surrendering eyes. He looked past her and made a gesture, jerking his chin at the door. She heard it open and close as the guards left. She gazed at him, suggesting somehow that he was her savior, and she was infinitely grateful.

"Please," she said again. "Help me."

He stood and moved around the desk to stand in front of her. His breathing had become thick and heavy. She looked up into his face, appealing, surrendering to his masculinity.

"Stand," he said.

She stood, and allowed the blanket to drop from her shoulders. She trembled, her breathing became ragged. She told him with her eyes that she was fascinated, seduced by his power over her. He reached for her shoulders. She closed her eyes and leaned in toward him. With her left hand she gently slipped her fingers behind his belt buckle. Then she stepped back with her right foot and smashed the heel of her hand into the tip of his chin, forcing his head back and snapping the vertebra.

As she lowered his twitching body to the floor she moaned, as though with pleasure, to muffle the sound. Then, with quick, steady fingers she removed his shoes and socks, his pants and his shirt, and put them on, leaving his jacket on his chair. She put his Glock in her waistband and moaned loudly again, repeating, "Yes, yes, oh Colonel...!"

Once dressed, she pulled the Glock from her belt, ruffled her hair, left a few moments of silence, then moved to the door and opened it a couple of inches, concealing her body behind it. The two guards were there and turned to frown at her. Sobbing, she said, "Please come in, something has happened, I think the colonel is ill. He was...and then he just..."

She pulled the door open, still shielding herself with it, and the two guards rushed in. They stood staring down at the gaping, semi-naked corpse and she softly closed the door behind them. Holding the Glock in both hands, she spoke quietly in Farsi.

"One way or another I am going to die. If I shoot you, that will alert your buddies and they'll come storming in and kill me. If I don't kill you, you'll alert your buddies, they'll come storming in and kill me. So I have to decide, how do I want to die? Taking you bastards with me, or on my knees and begging." By the time she had finished they had turned and were gaping at her. She smiled, jerked her chin at the colonel and said, "What would your guess be?"

They both started shaking their heads. One of them was fat and older, and had dirty fingernails. He said, "No, lady, no. Is no necessary. Is OK, you stay calm..."

"Oh, I'm very calm. Put your hands up."

She shifted the gun to the younger, thinner cop, took a step forward and smashed her instep into the fat guy's groin. He squeaked and wept and went down on his knees. The veins in his neck swelled and his face went crimson. Then he keeled over into the fetal position. She snapped at the younger cop, "Take his bootlaces."

He dithered and hesitated, then dropped to his knees and started undoing his pal's laces. Gallin didn't hesitate. She smashed her heel into his temple. His eyes rolled but stayed open and he rolled on his side.

She bent and took the magazine from his weapon. "What the hell would I want his laces for, stupid?" She stamped on the fat cop's neck. "Nobody gets out of this one alive." She took his magazine too, dropped them both in her pocket, concealed the Glock under her shirt and, with her heart pounding high in her chest, stepped out into the corridor. There was no one there. At the end of the passage to her left there was a staircase. She could see sunlight reflected on the wall of the stairwell, and she could hear voices rising from below, chatting, laughing.

She stepped back into the colonel's office, grabbed his wastepaper basket and stuffed it full of paper. She shoved it under the bentwood chair and pushed the chair up against the desk. Then she searched the colonel's jacket pocket and found, as she knew she would, his disposable lighter. With that she set fire to the wastepaper bin, saw that it caught the thin wood of the chair and then stepped out into the passage again.

She moved to the top of the stairs and stood staring, frowning like she was worried, at the colonel's office. When smoke started to creep from under the door she screamed, "*Aatash! Aatash!*" which meant, "*Fire! Fire!*"

People, men and women, came scrambling out of various offices and stared at her. She pointed, semi hysterical, at the colonel's door and screamed again, "*Aatash! Aatash!*"

Suddenly there was a stampede. Men and women, in uniform and in plain clothes, rushed for the door. Boots tramped up the stairs, milling people jostled and pushed past her. If anyone wondered who the hell she was, evidently they thought it was a question that could wait until the colonel's office had been dealt with. She muttered something about getting a fire extinguisher and rushed down the stairs.

She erupted into the ground floor hollering and pointing back at the stairs, that there was a fire in the colonel's office, that they needed extinguishers. A man and two women were standing at their desks, gaping. She screamed, "*Run!*" at them and they bolted for the stairs. Gallin begged them to hurry and walked out of the front door, grabbing a long coat and a long scarf from the coat rack, both of which conformed to the Iranian laws regarding women's dress.

She found herself on a broad, busy street. It was late afternoon. The sun was low and the shadows were long. To her right the road continued straight as far as the eye could see. To her left there was a large intersection. She went that way at a purposeful walk. At the intersection she turned right and decided to follow a pattern of right-left-left-right for the next hour, keeping her head down and her hair covered, while she attempted to decide what to do.

She had a number of imperatives which she needed to address. The most urgent was to find a safe place where she could find food and somewhere to sleep. In a country like Iran that presented multiple problems. As a woman, if she strayed from the prescribed behavior and dress codes she would be noticed and reported straight away. And if she was seen out, unaccompanied at night, she might well be reported too. Especially as the cops would be scouring the town, looking for her. They were bound to have found the three bodies by now.

As if echoing her thoughts, a few moments later the sudden wail of sirens rose above the sounds of the traffic. Her instinct was to duck into a side street, but that was exactly where they would be looking for her. She stayed with the crowds and slowed her pace.

Her other imperative was to get the hell out of Iran. That would mean either crossing into Turkey in the north-west, or arranging a rescue. For that she would have to contact either the Institute or her father in London, and right now that was all but impossible.

After an hour's walking the sun was beginning to dip toward the horizon in the west and she found she was wandering toward the outskirts of the town, among rambling, disheveled streets with grocery stores selling local produce on practically every corner. In these neighborhoods everybody would know everybody else and she would be drawing attention. She saw the men in the cafes watching her, and the women, in their black, witches' shrouds, squinted at her from their doorways.

She turned and started to retrace her steps. Despair clutched at her belly for a few seconds, but she quelled it, telling herself an answer would soon present itself. After ten or fifteen minutes, as headlamps and streetlights began to wink on, she came out onto a broad road. It was a dual carriageway with a central reservation where palms and flowers had been allowed to fend for themselves for a little too long. There were a couple of bars and restaurants spilling lonely light onto empty forecourts, and scattered shops going about the slow business of closing up for the night. Desultory cars slipped by in a broken rhythm, apparently going nowhere.

She stood a moment on the corner, fully aware of all the things she shouldn't do, all the things that would draw attention to her, but unable to think of a single thing she should do. That was when a ten-year-old, black BMW slowed and stopped beside her. The window slid down and the driver, a man in his forties with a maturing belly and a bushy moustache, leaned across the passenger seat and addressed her in Farsi. Farsi was a language she had mastered when she was a kid. Her dad had made sure of that. The guy said, "Hi. You want some money?"

She approached the window demurely and leaned in. "To feed my children."

"Get in." She climbed into the car and smiled shyly at the driver. He said, "You are young and pretty, I will give you fifty thousand *rials* for a full job."

A couple of seconds of mental arithmetic told her that

fifty thousand *rials* was around fifteen cents. She looked sad and nodded. "Where can we go? Somewhere private..."

"Sure. We can go down to the beach. If you are really good I can make you my temporary wife." He grinned as they took off toward the coast. "You would like that, eh?"

She nodded. "That would be wonderful. We could sleep in a bed and I could make you very happy."

He laughed. "Good girl," he said, and patted her leg. "That's the attitude."

It took them no more than five minutes to reach a small circus at the end of the avenue. Here he turned left and they were suddenly on a rough track with trees on their left and sand and rocks on their right. Beyond them she could see the moon suspended over the Caspian Sea. Here he pulled off the road, killed the engine and the lights, and turned to leer at her.

"Take off your coat and your shirt."

"I have a better idea," she said, and put the weapon in his face. "You take yours off first. Pull your pants down and get out of the car. In that order."

His face sagged and his eyes bulged. She took the keys from the ignition, got out and walked around to cover him as he stumbled out with his pants around his ankles. He got to his feet, pulling his pants up, and she waved the gun toward the shore. "Down to the beach."

She followed him through the rocks to the sand. When he was a few feet from the water she said, "Give me your wallet, your ID, your cell and all your other personal belongings."

His voice came back, shrill as he placed the items on the

sand. "My cousin is in the police. You will be whipped for this. You filthy whore!"

She picked up the cell. "Sure. I'm trembling as we speak. Take all your clothes off."

He stripped, shivering and whimpering, and made a neat pile of his clothes beside him. She picked up his iPhone, thumbed the screen and made him look at it. When she was in she stood back and shot him in the back of the head, so that the exit wound would make his face unrecognizable.

Before she did anything else she scrolled to settings on the phone and added her own face to the unlocking procedure. Then she used his disposable lighter to remove his fingerprints, and rolled the body into the water. After that she took his possessions, pocketed his cash—about four million *rials*, or a hundred American dollars—and dumped the rest in the trunk of the car. Then she drove, with her heart pounding, short of breath, north and west, headed, toward Turkey, about five hundred miles away.

TEN

In London, Ahmed scowled. He scowled for a long while, staring out of his window at the small, triangular garden in the middle of the crossroads below. He wanted to know whom Captain Gallin had contacted, and how, and what she had told them.

Finally he picked up his cell and dialed a number. It rang twice and a nasal, upper-class English voice drawled, "Colonel, I've been expecting your call."

"What is the situation with Captain Gallin?"

"Straight to the point, eh? The last I heard she swears blind she is not Captain Gallin. We have her at a police barracks prison in Chalus, on the Caspian Sea. Colonel Behnam, an expert in interrogation, was dispatched from Tehran to interrogate her. That's all I know for now." There was a short pause. Then there was a subtle change in D'Arcy's voice. "You've been paid, why should you care anyway?"

"I want her dead."

"Why?"

"That is not your concern."

"On the contrary. I think your motivation is very much my concern."

"Your concern is that she is an enemy of Iran and the enemy of your masters. Now you have her, interrogate her and kill her."

D'Arcy's voice became frigid. "I don't take instructions from you, Colonel. Her ultimate fate, as I told you before, depends on the Iranian authorities. I have made my recommendations and that's the best I can do."

"She must not return to London, ever! For your sake as well as mine!"

"When I have any news, I will let you know. That's the best I can do."

He hung up, clenched his right fist into a tight ball and pounded the wall three times, slow and steady.

———

AUNT PEG WATCHED Sarah go through customs and passport control ahead of her, with a sick pit in her stomach. Sarah was naturally oblivious to this. All she was aware of was Ali and his big brown eyes. It didn't even cross her mind that he might be using her as a mule. He was not like that. "Not like that" had become her mantra. Whatever Aunt Peg said, Sarah came back with, "He's not like that, Aunt Peg," or "They're not like that, Aunt Peg," or "Islam is not like that, Aunt Peg!" And there would follow a lecture on what it, they or he was really like; a lecture learnt, memorized word for word, straight from the mouth of Ali. And, Aunt Peg had noticed, a lecture that was increasingly virulent, and aggressively anti-Semitic.

She had tried to ignore her niece all the way across the ocean, by either sleeping or reading. That seemed to have suited Sarah well enough. She had spent the entire journey dreaming, both awake and sleep, about her great new love, Ali.

Now they had landed at JFK and Aunt Peg watched her, with that sick pit in her stomach again, go through passport control for the second time, and observed, a little maliciously, the air of disdain with which she observed the airport officials, particularly those who were tall and fair. She suppressed the feeling of irritation, but heard the voice in her head state very clearly: "That girl is going to get herself into serious trouble if she does not snap out of it."

It was in that moment, she realized, when she thought back on it, that she made her decision. As she went through the barriers and hurried to catch up with Sarah, she glanced at the airport officials and cops as they went about their business. Anxiety welled inside her, and she didn't know if it was the thought of betraying her niece, the fear that Ali was using her, or, worst of all, both.

What if the talisman turned out to be some form of terrorist device—a vial of some deadly virus, a chemical or biological weapon? Sarah could go to jail for the rest of her life. But Peg could vouch for her. And, the thought struck her forcefully, that her word would carry that much more weight if she informed now rather than after. If there was a terrorist attack, and Sarah was traced as the person who brought the weapon into the country... Then she would be in real trouble.

She called out to her niece, "Sarah, honey!"

Sarah, a few paces ahead, stopped and looked back at her aunt with an expression that her aunt could only describe as impatient patience, sprinkled with condescension. Aunt Peg gestured back to the lavatories and mouthed, "I just have to pop in..." then added more loudly, "I'll meet you at the car."

Sarah repressed a sigh and smiled. "But we're going to see Raza, right?"

"Of course. I'll be right there."

Aunt Peg watched Sarah hurry away, dragging her case behind her on little wheels. She turned and walked quickly back to where she had seen a couple of cops. When she got there she found they had moved on. An irrational panic began to grip her insides and she looked around, scanning the crowd for anyone at all in a uniform. Then she saw them, dark blue shirts, dark blue pants, baseball caps and assault rifles. A man and a blonde woman with a ponytail. They were forty paces away and watching her with interest. She raised a hand in a half-hearted wave and hurried over to them. The woman addressed her as she approached.

"Are you OK, ma'am?"

"Yes, um, I don't know. I don't think so. It's my niece..."

"Have you lost her?"

"No, no. She's meeting me—I mean, I am meeting her at the car. Our car. In the parking lot."

"You can't find the parking lot?"

"No, it's not that..." She took a deep breath. "We've just arrived from Lebanon, from Beirut." The two of them looked at each other. As though by some silent communication, the woman spoke again, turning back to Aunt Peg. "Something happened in Beirut?"

"Yes, I think so. I have been agonizing over it since we left. He, Ali, my niece's boyfriend, he said it was an amulet." She had started to tremble. She closed her eyes and tried to remember. "He said it was a small, gold amulet that had belonged to his cousin's father's great-grandfather. I think I've got that right. It had been given to him by some holy man," she screwed up her eyes tight, "um...Ali ibn Abu Talib, and it's inscribed with some sacred words."

The blonde cop took a step closer to her. "Let me get this right, ma'am. This Ali, your niece's boyfriend, asked her to bring this amulet to the United States?"

"Yes! That's what I am telling you. And she is so besotted with him. I tried to tell her, but she said I was being paranoid. So she packed it in her luggage, and it's probably nothing, but, what if it *is* something."

"And where did he tell you to deliver this amulet?"

"To a man called Raza, in the Bronx, in New York."

"Where is your niece now?"

"Waiting for me in the parking lot."

"You had better come with us, ma'am."

"Where?"

"Just to the office here. We need you to talk to somebody."

They each took her gently by an arm and guided her toward a passage that led to offices beyond the main concourse. She looked back toward where she had last seen Sarah marching away, with her red suitcase.

"Sarah," she said, almost like an invocation. "She'll be expecting me. She'll wonder what's happened to me."

"This won't take long, ma'am."

The male officer made a call on his radio and they led her

to an unmarked office beyond the public lavatories. There was a desk with a young man sitting at it who didn't acknowledge her existence. They led her past him, through a door and into a small room that looked unsettlingly like a police interrogation room. There was a Formica table with two chairs, a video camera mounted on the wall and a small microphone built into the table. They asked for her passport, took it and left her sitting at the table, wondering if she had been arrested, and beginning seriously to regret the decision she had taken.

Five minutes went by and a man in a denim shirt with a well trimmed blond beard and friendly blue eyes came in with two paper cups of coffee and several sachets and plastic containers of sugar and milk. He smiled at her as he set the stuff down.

"Detective Jim Harrington, Border Police. You are Peggy Anderson, of Bridgeport, Connecticut?"

"Yes, that's correct. But I am getting worried about my niece. She must be wondering where I am."

"Your niece is Sarah Crane, also of Bridgeport, Connecticut?"

"Yes."

He smiled reassuringly. "Don't worry. We are keeping an eye on her. She is in her car, on the phone. We won't keep you long. Can you just run through, for me, what happened in Beirut?"

She told him. At first she was halting and hesitant, inhibited by the appalling feeling that she was somehow betraying Sarah, her sister's daughter, and by the anxiety that Sarah might find out what she had done. But pretty soon she began to warm to her subject, and soon all her frustration and anger began to spill out as she told how Ali had homed in on them as they descended from the plane, how he had offered to help with their bags, getting them a taxi and finding them a better hotel. How he had become offended and angry when they had tried to pay him for his services, and had mellowed only when Sarah asked if they could at least invite him to dinner.

"He gate crashed every party after that, turning up at breakfast, inviting us to lunch, muscling in on dinner, and, putting it bluntly, seducing Sarah. He got her hooked and just reeled her in. Well, *at first* I thought he was just seducing her."

Detective Harrington nodded. "But then?"

"When he asked her to smuggle..." She faltered. "Well, we didn't see it as smuggling at the time. Really he just asked us to deliver this amulet to his cousin's son. And Sarah believed his story and I guess, right then, I did. But after he had gone, the more I thought about it, the more uncomfortable I became. Until when we touched down I just couldn't stand it anymore. I told her to go on to the car and I was going to the bathroom, and I came to look for you."

He nodded for a bit, then said, "You probably did the right thing. It probably is nothing more than a gift for his son, but you can't be too careful. Look, we don't want to cause unnecessary stress. Here is what we'll do. I'll have you sign this statement which you've made, which is being automatically transcribed by the magic of modern technology, even as we speak. And, if you can give us the address where you are supposed to deliver this gift, we'll take care of things."

Aunt Peg raised her eyebrows. "You're not going to look at what's in the package?"

"We don't want to cause any unnecessary distress, Ms. Anderson. If you'll just deliver the package as arranged, and then go on your way home, that will be fine."

"Oh…"

He gave a small laugh. "Don't worry, we take what you've told us very seriously. We'd just rather have you safely at home before we take any action." He paused a moment. "There is just one thing. Would you say that your niece has become sympathetic to the Muslim cause?"

Tears welled in Aunt Peg's eyes. "You know young idealists, searching for a cause. This week it's polar bears, next week it's world poverty, especially when they're in love…"

He nodded. "Sure, let's hope she moves on to free speech and human rights before too long."

Aunt Peg smiled and nodded. "Yes, let's hope so."

She wrote down the address Ali had given them, and then hurried through the airport to the parking lot.

When she reached the car Sarah was still on the phone. Aunt Peg climbed in as she was saying, "OK, Aunty is back *at last!* Gotta go." There was a brief pause, then, "No, no, no problems at all." Another pause. "Just Aunty getting old and needing to go peepee!"

She hooted with laughter at this, they exchanged embarrassing endearments and farewell kisses and she finally hung up. Aunt Peg looked at her and silently promised herself it would be a good, long time before she saw her niece again.

"Can we get this done, honey? I am dying to get home and put my feet up."

Sarah's voice was terse as she pressed the starter button.

"Sure, but if they invite us in for tea or something, we have to accept. You know in Muslim culture they would be very offended if we said no."

Anger suddenly flared up in Aunt Peg's belly. "And in American culture it would be considered very offensive to keep a sixty-year-old woman on her feet and hanging around after a fifteen-hour flight! And if they choose to come and live in America, let them learn our damn customs!"

She crossed her arms and stared furiously out of the windshield. Sarah gasped and stared at her aunt. After a moment she pulled out of the lot and headed north, toward Whitestone Bridge and the Bronx. They drove in silence as the sun slipped down toward the horizon and the air turned grainy.

When they were over the East River, Sarah suddenly blurted out, "I am *so* disappointed! If I had known you were so prejudiced, and...and *racist!* I would never have asked you to come on this trip." Her aunt didn't answer, so she went on. "How can you be so *awful* about those *beautiful* people? They are so gentle and kind and hospitable."

"Stop! I have reached the end of my patience, Sarah. I have put up with enough for the last week! And I am frankly sick and tired of hearing how damned wonderful *they* are and how damned *awful* we are! So cut it out!"

They continued in silence over the black water toward the flickering lights of Westchester Creek and Throgs Neck. Then Aunt Peg frowned and turned to her sulking niece.

"If you hadn't gone with me, who *would* you have gone with?"

"No one."

"You would have gone *alone*, to *Lebanon?*"

"Why not?"

"You wouldn't go alone to Wal-Mart, let alone Lebanon!" Sarah said nothing, but directed a defiant face at the road. Aunt Peg turned slowly in her seat to face her niece more fully. The awful realization was dawning on her. Her heart was pounding and her face was hot and red. "You already knew him!" No reply. "How? How did you meet..." She put her hands to her mouth. "Oh my God, Sarah, what have you done? You met him online!"

Sarah screwed up her face and half-shouted. "Oh, for God's sake, Aunt Peg! This is the twenty-first century, for crying out loud! You don't have to wait to be formally introduced anymore, you know! People meet online all the time!"

Aunt Peg leaned back in her seat with a sudden feeling of dread slowly enveloping her. The apparent chance meeting with Ali, the way they both seemed already to know each other, the eagerness to help by bringing the package, and even, she realized with deepening terror, the polite ease with which Detective Harrison had allowed her to leave without looking at the gift they had brought for Raza.

She drew breath to tell Sarah they must throw the gift away and head directly for home. But no sooner had the thought crossed her mind than she remembered that Ali had Sarah's address and hers. And so did the cops.

They had no choice but to see it through.

Through to the bitter end.

ELEVEN

I was collected from the airport in a dark blue Audi by a chauffer who was about as cheerful as a hangover on a Monday morning in January. It was a forty-five-minute drive from the Imam Khomeni International Airport, about twenty-five miles southwest of downtown Tehran, to my hotel. The hotel was the Espinas International, and to say it was extravagantly opulent would be unfair to extravagant opulence. It was the kind of palace Aladdin might have ordered from his jinn if he'd really let his inhibitions go. Of course there was no bar and no alcohol, and if there had been, you'd have been very unlikely to meet an interesting woman within the former or consuming the latter. So I checked in, was told I had no messages, and had a bellhop take my bags up to my room. I gave him ten bucks—or four hundred and twenty-two thousand, five hundred *rial*—and had a long shower.

When I was done I called the number D'Arcy had given me to contact my liaison when I arrived. The cell was one I had been given to use in Iran. The one I had to communicate with ODIN was in a small, lead-lined compartment in the bottom of one of my bags, in case I needed it for a rapid extraction. After a couple of rings the phone was answered by a nice female voice with enough of an accent to be exotic.

"Dr. Dana Zamanian."

Good evening, Doctor. This is Dr. Henry Bassett. I believe you are to be..."

"Indeed, Dr. Bassett. I am. Let me ask you first and foremost if you are happy and comfortable in the hotel we have chosen for you."

"Only a dry martini could make it any better."

The smile in her voice was more tolerant than amused.

"I am afraid that is not possible, Dr. Bassett. Are you free this evening to discuss the next stage of your integration into the program?"

"I am ready when you are, and at your complete disposal." I was visualizing Gal Gadot on the other end of the line, reclining on a gilt *chaise lounge* with a six-inch cigarette holder between her teeth, and I was getting into the spirit of the thing.

"I shall be there in twenty minutes and we shall dine together. Will you please meet me in the lobby?"

"That sounds perfect," I said, and couldn't help wondering if she looked as good as she sounded; not that I tried very hard.

I shaved and was not mean with the aftershave, dressed elegantly masculine and made my way to the lobby. Dr. Dana Zamanian arrived dead on time five minutes later. She wore a floor-length lavender gown with a purple shawl over her hair, which was about as black as hair can get without sucking in light and small planets. Her eyes were black and her lips were extravagantly red. She was way over the top, but looked every bit as good as she sounded. Except for the small matter of the complete lack of expression on her face, and her face. It made her look sultry. Sultry was pretty good, but a smile would have taken her beyond beautiful.

She stood six feet from me and said, "Covid is rampant here, Doctor, I hope you don't mind if we don't touch."

"That damned Covid. Where would you like to eat?"

"Right here." She turned and walked on rapid feet toward the dining room, forcing me to skip a couple of steps to catch up as she spoke over her shoulder. "I imagine Sir Leo has told you something of our project, but if you don't mind I will take it from the top to make sure you have all the details."

I followed her into a magnificent, palatial dining room, muttering something about that being fine. The maître obviously knew her, because he snatched up a couple of menus, bowed like she was the queen of Sheba, said, "Dr. Zamanian, an honor!" and hurried to pull her chair out for her.

I was clearly not an honor because I had to pull my own chair and sit unassisted. She snapped something in Farsi and he went away.

"I have ordered *fesenjan* to start. This is walnuts, pomegranate paste and duck soup. Then *ghormeh sabzi* for the main course. Many herbs, kidney beans and lamb. You will like it. We will drink water."

I was getting tired of telling her what she did was excellent. So I just smiled and waited.

"You must have an early night, tonight, Dr. Bassett. You will have a very early start in the morning."

"What happens if I am naughty and stay awake till after midnight? Will you be checking on me?"

"No. The car will come to collect you at six in the morning. So you must be up and packed, and having breakfast at five. This project is military project and you must follow military discipline."

I smiled. "I must have missed that part in the contract I signed with Sir Leo."

She raised an exotic eyebrow. "That is a problem?"

"I'm not a soldier."

"But you receive exceptionally high pay for your service. That pay means, during contract, you submit to Iranian law. Iranian law says, on this project you are under the jurisdiction of army."

"Then I guess it's not a problem."

The waiter came with a bottle of water and two bowls of mulberry red soup. He poured the water and left.

"You would be wise, Dr. Bassett, to take this seriously."

"I take it very seriously, believe me. What else do I need to know?"

She took a couple of spoonfuls of soup and dabbed at her mouth with her napkin. There was something feline about her movements.

"You will be six months at the facility."

"Where's that?"

"I don't know. You will not leave the facility. You will be confined. Anything you need, food, drink, women, anything, you inform the facility director, and he will provide it for you every Thursday. After six months you have one week in Tehran and then return to the facility."

"Wow, that's pretty intense."

"Intense is what we need, Dr. Bassett. We are in a hurry."

I ate soup for a bit, glancing at her in between spoonfuls. Finally I set down the spoon and asked, "For what"

The look she flashed me made no pretence at not being hostile.

"For getting the program finished, obviously."

"Why the hurry?"

"That is a political question, Dr. Bassett, and not your concern."

I held up my hands. "My apologies. It was not my intention to intrude." I tried a friendly smile. "Sometimes if you know the motivation, it can become infectious."

"Western bullshit. Here, you are told to do the job, and you do the job. That is your motivation."

"That can work too. Are there any other Americans on the team?"

My hope, a forlorn one, was that asking about Americans would be seen as a natural enough question, but might lead her to mention other foreigners too, which might just give me something about Gallin.

"You will meet your team tomorrow."

Like I said, it was a forlorn hope. The waiter came and took away the soup bowls, while another delivered the lamb. Dana refilled our glasses and the waiters left us alone again.

"Dr. Bassett, I must ask you a personal question."

"Shoot."

"What is your feeling about Jews, and Israel."

I chewed and gave her a lopsided smile at the same time.

"I read the papers, Dr. Zamanian, and I know if I tell you I am very sympathetic to the Israeli situation, I'll be on the next plane back to New York. But then, on the other hand, if I were sympathetic to Israel and the Jews, I wouldn't be doing this job in the first place, would I?"

"Why?" She didn't look at me when she asked. She had her eyes firmly on her food.

"Why?" I was genuinely surprised. "I am being employed by your AEOI. That's the Atomic Energy Organization of Iran. But I am not a nuclear physicist. I'm a rocket scientist. My specialization is delivery systems. Let's not be cute. That means I am here to enable you to deliver a nuclear warhead to a selected enemy. Iran's number-one declared enemy is Israel, and Iran has clearly stated its intention to wipe Israel off the map. That's what we call a no-brainer."

"And how would you feel, Dr. Bassett, knowing that your rocket design had been responsible for annihilating nearly seven million people, and exterminating the Jewish homeland?"

I shook my head. "Uh-uh, no you don't. I design rockets and delivery systems, and I am pretty damned good at it. What you choose to put on the nose, and where you choose to send it in the future, that, my friend, is your karma, not mine."

I tucked smugly into the lamb and kidney beans. She watched me do it for a moment, then took a dainty piece of lamb on her fork and put it in her mouth.

"Of course, it is easy to take that attitude when we can displace the event into the future. But what if it was not so far in the future?"

I sat back in my chair. Inside, wild alarm bells were

ringing but I managed to smile skeptically at her while I dabbed my mouth.

"You're out of your mind," I told her. "The United States would retaliate. The whole Western World would march in..."

She laughed for the first time. I had been wrong. It did not make her beautiful. It made her ugly in ways I could not describe.

"The United States?" Her eyebrows were arched high, incredulous. "Come, Mr. Mason, you know as well as I do that the American Empire is in decline, and dear Mr. Biden is old and decrepit, and has no stomach for a fight. He has pulled out of Afghanistan and if he could he would pull out of NATO. Besides—" She sipped her water, watching me across the table. "When presented with the *fait accompli*," she pronounced it with a flawless French accent, "what can they do? Nuke us?"

I had stopped looking skeptical and I was listening seriously to what she was saying. I shrugged to signal I didn't care what they did, but added, "They didn't nuke Saddam Hussein, or bin Laden..."

She cut me short with another ugly laugh. "That was 1990, when America was governed by George Bush senior. He was strong leader." She leaned forward and pointed a finger at me like a pistol. "But even then, notice how they did not finish the job. They had to come back, with George Bush son, and Tony Blair, pretending there were weapons of mass destruction. Why? Because Western politics is crippled by public opinion. And bin Laden? Ha! Let me remind you, Dr. Bassett, that Afghanistan is America's second Vietnam. Bin Laden died, but the Taliban won."

I was quiet for a long moment. I tried to hide my astonishment by smiling and shaking my head.

"You can't be serious."

"Of course I am serious. Tell me, what can the West do? Economic sanctions? We already have economic sanctions. Poverty is so severe here that men are sending out their wives as prostitutes for fifty, sixty cents a job. Iran has more prostitutes than any country on earth. Did you know that? You want a whore?"

"No, thanks."

"It will cost you sixteen cents. Any street corner."

"Thanks, I'm good. Getting back to a nuclear strike on Israel..."

"So, what? A retaliatory strike on Iran? How many innocent people will die in such a strike? There are more than eight million people in Tehran. Maybe one million will die from the explosion. The rest will die from radiation poisoning, which will fall out all over the Middle East and Asia." She began to list on her fingers, "Iraq, Syria, Turkey, Afghanistan, Pakistan, Turkmenistan, Azerbaijan, Georgia, Russia..." She smiled and arched an eyebrow. "You think Biden is man enough to do this? You think he has...?" She held her hands out, palm up, like two claws holding a couple of coconuts.

"Retaliation does not have to be nuclear," I said, trying to ignore the imagery she had conjured. "You would have all of the Middle East against you, not to mention the USA, NATO, Great Britain, the European Union—"

"You think so?"

"Of course."

"With a nuclear arsenal? And having shown we are

prepared to use it? Whom shall we send the next missile to? Rome? Paris? Brussels? London? New York? Washington? Or shall we send three—to the Brussels Stock Exchange, the London Stock Exchange and Wall Street? Yes, I think that is a good plan." She shook her head. "But that will never happen, Dr. Bassett, because nobody will retaliate. When you have a nuclear weapon, and you are ready to use it, people don't retaliate. They open the doors and let you into the club, like China, like India, like Russia."

"Holy cow, you really are serious."

"Yes, Dr. Bassett, I really am serious. And if I have been a little rude this evening, it is because I was not told to receive you and make you comfortable. That is the job of the hotel. I was told to make you aware of the nature of the job you have taken on. Saddam Hussein's big mistake was that he acted too soon. If he had waited until he had an atomic arsenal, they would never have invaded Iraq. We are not so stupid." Contempt twisted her mouth into an ugly sneer. "We are not Arabs, Dr. Bassett. We will not make the same mistake."

The waiter came and withdrew our plates. She snapped something at him which I took to mean coffee, he bowed and went away. She went on, a little less aggressively.

"Understand, Dr. Bassett, that you are part of a project which is the culmination of our destiny. While you are in our employ, you will obey without question. Punishment for disobedience will be severe and without trial. Is all of this clear to you?"

"Yes," I said and gave my head a small shake. "But I hope the rewards will make up for it. You're trying hard to scare me, but I am not scared. I am not a hero or a savior. I'm here to do a job and get paid. I'll keep my head down for the next three years and do as I'm told. The rest is up to you."

"Admirable." She said it with heavy sarcasm and plenty of contempt.

"Hey." I shrugged and leaned back so the waiter could deliver the coffee. "Adapt and survive. I'm a survivor."

She didn't look impressed. "You replace Dr. Enzo Benini. He had a problem with talking. He talked all the time, and all the time he was complaining. When he discovered the nature of the program which I have just explained to you, he expressed his opinion that it was inhuman. The director of the facility explained to him that we were not exterminating human beings. We were exterminating Jews. This made him crazy. So we exterminated him."

"You made your point, Dr. Zamanian."

"We have been recruiting to find a replacement for him. Other people have applied. Some of them were not good enough, some of them were spies for Israel. Those we exterminated too. Do your job, obey the rules, and in thirty-six months you will be a very rich, happy man."

"I understand. I have no opinion to express, and I love keeping a low profile and working."

"That is good for you. Do not get up. Enjoy your coffee."

She stood and swept out of the dining room like a beautiful vision from a grotesque horror movie.

TWELVE

THE NEXT MORNING I WAS IN THE LOBBY AT FIVE fifty-five, and at six on the button a large man in a badly cut blue suit pushed through the glass doors. He had a black beard the size of his head, a nose like a talon and eyes so black you could lose your soul in them. He stood at the door and looked around. He saw me sitting and watching him and approached me.

"You are Dr. Bassett."

It wasn't a question but I said, "I am."

"Come. I have car for you."

Like Dr. Dana Zamanian, he was not here to make me comfortable. He turned and walked away. I carried my cases after him into the black morning. He opened the trunk of a large, dark Mercedes and I slung my cases in. He slammed it shut and it sounded uncomfortably like a gunshot in the predawn. I climbed in the back and before I could close the door he was making the wheels complain as we took off into the silent city.

We fishtailed into Versal Shirazi Street, a broad avenue with five-storey blocks that had been modern in the '70s. It was dark and empty and we did at least sixty all the way to the intersection with Enghelab Street. The lights were red, but he didn't care. He didn't so much brake as play footsie with the pedal for a second and skid round the corner into the four-lane avenue.

A few of the grocery stores were pulling up their blinds, spilling dull light onto the street. But aside from that the road was empty and dark. Now it was a straight line for over three miles to the huge circus called Azadi Square, with the grotesque Azadi Tower at its center. He put his foot down and the car surged. We hit the circus and drifted, screaming, for almost half a mile around the broad bend, then rocketed out through Meraj Boulevard where he braked by dropping down through the gears and suddenly we were at the Mehrabad Domestic Airport.

He said, "You come."

I followed him into the main concourse, through security—where he showed a pass and said something guttural—and down a long, tiled passage out onto the tarmac. There a Dassault Falcon 7X was waiting with the steps lowered and the cabin lights reflect on the black asphalt. Grumpy pointed and wagged his huge beard as he said, "You go."

I smiled. "But Rick," I said, "what about us?"

He scowled darkly, jerked his head at the plane and insisted, "You go, now!"

"I guess we'll always have Paris, huh?" I tightened my grip on my cases and made for the plane. "Here's lookin' at you, kid!" I called back, but he was already disappearing back through the security doors.

The jet was not what I had expected. It was furnished with leather armchairs, a sofa and fold-down, highly polished walnut tables. I stowed my luggage by the door and sat at one of those tables. I thought maybe a pretty hostess might come and offer me coffee and croissants, but nothing like that happened. Instead, a miserable guy in a blue uniform and a pencil moustache emerged from the cockpit, pretended not to see me, closed the door and returned to the cockpit, where he closed that door too. A moment later we began to taxi toward the runway, and five minutes after that we were hurtling through the early predawn along the black strip. We lurched, jumped, and then we were rising, soaring high above the city with the small, twinkling lights falling away beneath us. We banked left, south, and soon we were over the desert. All the lights vanished one by one and below us there was only an impenetrable blackness.

Nothing much happened after that, so I dozed for an hour and eventually we began to descend. As we banked I looked out the window and saw we were approaching a military airbase. I also saw out to the east the graying of the horizon behind high, barren mountains.

Ten minutes later we had touched down and were taxiing past six Mig 29s and a couple of Iranian HESA Azarakhsh. After a short while we came to a halt outside a couple of large hangars, a hundred yards or so from the main complex of buildings and offices. The pilot stepped out of the cockpit and ignored me again. He opened the door, lowered the stairs, saluted and stepped back.

I waited, and after a couple of seconds a tall, balding man in a suit stepped through the door and smiled at me. I returned the smile and stood. That must have encouraged him because he held out both hands and said, "Dr. Bassett. Welcome to Shiraz!"

"Thank you, Mr...?"

"Abdul, simply Mr. Abdul." He spread his hands in a kind of apology. "I must insist on the 'Mister' to maintain respect among the other workers. I know in America you are more relaxed about this kind of thing."

I gave him a smile that was completely devoid of feeling and said, "As long as you call me Dr. Bassett and don't start calling me Hey You, it's not a problem for me."

We both laughed like I'd said something hilarious. A couple of grunts in uniform appeared and grabbed my cases, and Mr. Abdul led me off the plane, talking over his shoulder as he went. "You must be hungry, Dr. Bassett, and in need of coffee. I apologize for the early start, but we are in something of a hurry."

I tramped down the steps after him into the paling dawn. "So Dr. Zamanian told me last night. She said you would explain the need for haste."

He glanced at me, like it was a question. I ignored the question on his face and looked around. We were on a sandy, dusty plateau just behind nowhere and slightly to the left of the back of beyond. There were burnt ochre mountains in the distance on every side and desiccated earth everywhere. Remote was busy and overcrowded compared to Shiraz.

I returned my gaze to his face, gave him a lopsided smile and shrugged. "Not that I am bothered. I'm here to do my job and get paid. But personally I prefer to get involved as much as I can. It helps to get motivated."

He nodded like he understood. It was the kind of gesture that suggested he had studied in the West and knew all about our decadent theories.

"Yes, I know that is the way you do things. We do things a little differently, but don't worry, Dr. Bassett. You will get plenty of motivation." He turned and moved on. "We have a bit of a drive ahead of us still I am afraid, but it will give us an opportunity to get to know each other, and I can answer any questions you might have."

We followed a path through a security gate to a parking lot that had only a handful of vehicles in it. Abdul led me to a two-year-old Range Rover which bleeped as we approached, and we both climbed in. He fired up the engine, spun the wheel and we exited the airbase gates, headed north and a little west, toward the mountains, some three or four miles away.

When we were under way I said, "I don't really have any questions, to tell you the truth, Mr. Abdul. And Dr. Zamanian made it pretty clear to me last night that questions would not be all that welcome. She also said this facility was run pretty much on a military basis." I gave my head a little shake. "I have no political convictions, I am not a hero and I make no pretence at having a restless conscience. All I want is to do my job—" I glanced at him. "I like my job, and I like to do it well." I shrugged and gave a small laugh. "And most of all, I want to get paid."

"An admirable attitude."

His face said he wasn't being sarcastic. I added, "But I guess I am a little concerned about one thing..."

"And what is that?"

"Comfort. All this military drill, up at five in the morning, in the lobby by six sharp, on site for six months at a time…" I shook my head. "I asked Dr. Zamanian if there were any other Americans on the team and she almost had me arrested as a spy."

He threw back his head and roared with laughter. "Dana! She is a fearsome lady and you would be very wise not to get on her bad side. I won't say stay on her good side, because she hasn't got one!" He laughed again. "But she tends to overstate things. I think she would have been happier in the Third Reich than in Iran."

He chuckled for a bit as we drove through the dusty streets of low-rise blocks that served as a dormitory town for the airbase.

"But it is true," he went on more seriously, "that it is best not to display too much curiosity. I myself am of a relaxed disposition. I imagine your question had more to do with socializing than anything else. But there are officers and administrators who are highly suspicious of our American and European scientists."

"Not more," I said, "*everything* to do with socializing and unwinding. She had just told me we would be confined to the facility for six months at a time. However dedicated you are, in that kind of confinement, you start to get pretty homesick for familiar voices and customs."

He nodded and shrugged. "Naturally."

I pressed him a little further. "So I gather there *are* some Americans at the facility—or at least English speakers."

"Yes, oh yes, English speakers. You will meet them presently. It's a shame. We had a rather attractive English woman who was going to join us, but it didn't work out."

"Shame." I laughed, feeling a hot jolt in my gut. "Even if

she wasn't qualified, this desert must get pretty wearing after a while. At least she would have been something pretty to look at."

It was subtle and he didn't seem to pick up that I was fishing.

"Ha!" he said. "Indeed, but it wasn't her qualifications that were the issue. She was Jewish."

"Oh," I said, like I wasn't interested, trying hard to stifle the burn in my belly. "So her resumé went in the recycling bin."

"Oh no," he gave a dry, humorless laugh, "be warned. She was arrested and sent for interrogation. The immediate —and natural—assumption was that she was an Israeli spy. I hope you have no Jewish connections, Dr. Barrett. They are not tolerated here."

"Me?" I said, like I didn't give a damn about the girl. "Nah, American Anglo-Saxon stock all the way back to King Canute."

He glanced at me briefly and his face suggested that American Anglo-Saxon wasn't all that much better than Jewish. In the silence that followed I gazed out the side window, trying hard to suppress the twisting anxiety in my belly. She had applied, and she had been betrayed, as I had suspected. She had not been killed in London, but I still had no idea whether she had been executed here; whether they had chosen to make an example of her.

We left the town and drove through harsh, unforgiving desert. Red, ochre and yellow dust spread out as far as you could see in all directions, with small fields of exhausted, struggling crops scattered here and there among shacks and small houses where life was born and withered without ever knowing anything but the desert.

Eventually we came to a fork in the road. The left fork continued straight on, but the right fork turned in among steep escarpments, following the course of a deep canyon. Steadily, but painfully slowly, we ascended toward the highlands above.

We didn't talk much for the rest of the journey. I didn't want to arouse his suspicions by asking any more questions, and he seemed preoccupied with the narrow hairpins in the dirt track that passed for a road. So I closed my eyes and tried to reason out what had happened to Gallin.

I was eventually brought back from my thoughts by the subtle change in the movement of the truck, and the change of the sound of the engine from a grinding whine, to an easier hum. We had stopped climbing and hit a straight road, and now we were accelerating.

I opened my eyes and saw a landscape that might have been the surface of Mars. We were on a high tableland of red rock and dust as far as the eye could see. Here, the road was asphalt once again and cut like a black scar through the alien wasteland; and we were speeding along it toward what looked like a massive red wall, a fortress of rusty stone rising two hundred feet into the air, some two or three miles away.

In the center of that wall there was a deep, jagged split, as though some angry god had struck it with an axe, splitting the towering cliff in two halves. And the long, straight, black ribbon of the road plunged right into that split.

Abdul glanced at me and smiled. "We are here."

I nodded ahead. "In there?"

"Yes, it is a very secure location."

"It's superb. Not even the satellites could see you in there."

"Correct," he said, with a little, self-satisfied smirk.

Pretty soon we were in among the sheer, soaring walls, no more than thirty or forty paces apart at the entrance, but widening steadily until we arrived at what could only be described as the bottom of a vast well, or chimney. Above us was a broad, rough circle of red cliffs, framing a perfectly blue sky. And all around us was the deep shade cast by those massive rock walls, and in those deep shadows, at the very base of the cliffs, were a jumble of prefabricated buildings, two and three stories high, painted with sand-textured stone red and ochre paint, making them invisible to aircraft or satellites above.

I made no effort to hide my incredulity. I raised my eyebrows and pointed at the prefabs.

"This is your atomic research facility?"

He shook his head. "No, Dr. Bassett. The research facility is *inside* the cliffs. The *doors* are inside the prefabs." He laughed and shook his head, somehow managing to convey how naïve Americans were when it came to Iran. We swung down from the truck and he put his hand on my shoulder to guide me toward the largest of the prefabs, where a couple of soldiers with assault rifles had stepped out and held the door open for us. Abdul did not acknowledge them, but spoke to me as we walked.

"Persia was once the greatest of all superpowers, you know, Dr. Bassett. In fact we were the first superpower on this planet."

"Sumeria. I thought that was Iraq."

He shrugged, pulling the corners of his mouth down and spreading his hands. "Sumeria, Mesopotamia, it straddled the Euphrates and the Tigris as far as the Karun River, and took in the whole northern coast of the Gulf, from Kuwait to Gachsaran." He laughed. "We are talking about the time before history, when the gods themselves came down from the sky to create man in *Edin*, the plains at the mouth of the two rivers. In those days they didn't know that if they were on that side of the Tigris they were Iraqi. All they knew was to serve their gods, the Anunnaki."

He stopped with one foot in the door and put his hand on my shoulder.

"What I am saying is that we have been here a long time, we have been around the block, as you say, and we know something about accruing, keeping and *using* power."

I closed my eyes and nodded like I had been put in my place and understood. I refrained from asking how that had worked for them over the last thousand years. I didn't think he'd appreciate that question.

He went inside and I followed him.

We were in a large, cavernous hangar-like building, like a giant, metal shipping container. The ceiling and three walls were of steel, but the far wall was sheer rock. In the center of that rock there was a concrete frame and, held in the frame, was a steel door.

"We did not tunnel from scratch," he told me. "We took advantage of a cave system that was already here, simply expanded it where necessary and constructed living quarters, a barracks, and the laboratories. Oddly enough," he laughed, "the most difficult thing was installing plumbing!"

The steel doors started to roll back, raising a tremendous

metallic racket, forcing him to step closer to me and raise his voice.

"Some of the caves to the south, adjacent to your rocketry lab, were nearly vertical and we were able to exploit them as silos."

"For the rockets," I said. He nodded. "For the rockets."

THIRTEEN

IT WAS NOT UNLIKE SIMILAR FACILITIES THAT I HAD seen in Nevada and New Mexico. Until you see it you think it's like something out of a James Bond movie, but when you actually get inside one of those facilities, you realize it's just your bog-standard military base put inside a mountain, so prying satellites and high-flying drones can't see you. The Iranians knew that if they pursued their nuclear program out in the open, either the US or the Israelis—or both— would take out their facilities at the first whiff of weapons- grade plutonium. But under half a mile of mountain, with the regime virtually cut off from the world, their progress had become almost completely undetectable.

Beside the entrance there were half a dozen buggies parked like shopping carts in an area of black and yellow chevrons. A couple of grunts brought in my cases and slung them in the back of a buggy, then drove us a short distance down concrete passages populated by occasional, anony- mous doors.

"Most of these are administrative offices," Abdul explained. "The barracks are nearer the entrance. And right at the back are the scientists' and engineers' quarters, on the third and fourth floor. On the first and second floor are the nuclear laboratories, dining room, common room and bar. Your lab is in the basement, over on the right, to the south." He glanced at me and laughed. "Yes, we have a well-stocked bar, and on Thursdays we bring up nice girls from Dashtak. They are very sweet."

I made a rapid calculation in my head. Today was Tuesday and I had a pretty strong feeling that by Thursday I would be either gone or dead.

We ascended to the fourth floor in an elevator, took another buggy and pulled up outside an anonymous door. The soldiers jumped down, grabbed my cases, and carried them inside. I climbed out of the buggy and Abdul told me, "I'll give you half an hour to settle in, then I'll collect you, give you the tour, introduce you to your colleagues. After that we'll have a little chat in my office about what we expect from you."

He departed with the soldiers and I went inside. It was basic, not exactly what Sir Leo D'Arcy had led me to believe: a steel-framed bed with rough blankets and sheets, a melamine wardrobe and chest of drawers. There was also a desk with a computer terminal and a printer. Through an arch beyond the bed there was a basic bathroom with a shower cubicle.

I unpacked my stuff, had a quick shower and changed into fresh clothes, and five minutes after that Abdul arrived to take me on my tour of the facility. I am no expert on nuclear science or atomic bombs, and what I know about rocket science was pretty much what I learned as a kid—light the fuse and run; plus what the Chief had given me to read and memorize a couple of days earlier. So I tried to look intelligent for an hour or so, nodded a lot and made pertinent comments as Abdul showed me around the setup. We visited the labs, including the one that was to be mine, and he introduced me to a couple of section supervisors. He told me to talk to them if I needed anything. There didn't seem to be any scientists or engineers around and eventually I asked him about that.

"They are waiting for us in the meeting room. There I will introduce you to each member of the teem, and clarify for you exactly what it is I need from you."

It was the second time he had said that, but I was beginning to get a pretty good idea what that was anyway.

Eventually we left the main plutonium processing plant and made our way down a short corridor where there was a single door. Abdul pushed through and held it open for me to enter. The room was about twenty foot square, with plain white walls and a large, oval, walnut table in the center. There were a dozen chairs around it, none of which were occupied. There were also a couple of sofas against the far wall, some mismatched armchairs and a couple of coffee tables. Unlike the table, the chairs and the sofas were occupied, by five guys who were all looking at me. Their faces were not exactly hostile, but they weren't exactly pulling out the cold beers either.

They were a mixed bunch. There was a young guy in his twenties. He looked skinny and unhappy and his wispy beard, black T-shirt and jeans seemed to hang from his bones like they were nostalgic for the days when they used to get washed. Abdul told me his name was Dr. Simon Hirsch. I told him hello, but he just stared at me from his chair like he was still sulking about when his mommy had told him no more Halo.

Next was a guy sitting on the arm of the sofa. His name was Dr. Borg Erickson. He was clean-cut, clean shaven and had a pipe in his mouth. He showed me the palm of his hand and said, "Hello."

Sitting on the sofa was a man in a white lab coat who looked like a dumpling wrapped in a white handkerchief. He was spherical and motley and in his sixties. His unhappy soul peered out through angry blue eyes that hid behind heavy, horn-rimmed glasses. His name was Dr. Peter Schneider.

"He is the program director and ultimately your instructions will come from him."

I nodded to him and asked, "Are you a nuclear physicist, Dr. Schneider, or a rocket scientist?"

He gave me a look like I'd made an inappropriate joke and said, "I heff zee IQ off one hundret unt sixty. I em a cosmologist. I do everysink!"

Beside him in an armchair was another geek I figured was Simon Hirsch's pal. He was large, had a black ponytail down to his ass and a beard which probably provided a safe environment for new kinds of fauna. His name was Paul Henley, but he didn't answer to that name. He just stared at his right knee.

The final member of the quintet was leaning against the wall by the window. He was dark and well groomed in chinos and a crisp blue shirt. His name was Dr. Pierre Blanchet. He bowed and spread his hands like there was nothing he could do about being called Pierre Blanchet.

"So," said Abdul, "these are your colleagues for the next three years. I hope you will be friends. I am sure they will help you in any way that they can. Are there any questions you wish to ask?"

"Yes." I nodded. "Will I be working directly with any one of you?"

Dr. Schneider answered. "You vill be verking mit all off us. But each one off us is in charge of one particular aspect off zee program. Your responsibility is zee rocket unt zee delivery system." He turned to Abdul. "You heff told him...?"

Abdul cut him short. "No. Not yet."

"Zen let me say, you vill not be verking *directly* mit us. But you vill heff your team off engineers."

Abdul added, "You will understand better after I have briefed you on the specifics of your job, Dr. Bassett."

Borg raised his pipe and spoke in almost perfect English. "My specialization is propulsion systems, Dr. Bassett. I imagine you and I will be working closely. Perhaps we can get together later for a drink, and I will put you up to speed on the kinds of propulsion we are working with."

"That would be very helpful, Dr. Erickson."

There was a little more toing and froing in which Drs. Henley and Hirsch did not participate, and Dr. Blanchet shrugged and said, "Voila!" three times. Finally Abdul concluded, "So, you will have plenty of opportunity to get to know each other better later on, now you and I must talk turkey!" He laughed uproariously, as though he had said something hilarious.

"Good," I said, "that's good. Talk turkey. I like it."

And we left.

Ten minutes later we were in his office. It was spartanly furnished, with a metal desk, a bookcase and a couple of filing cabinets, and, as with the other rooms, there were no windows, because we were deep inside the mountain. The feeling was oppressive and I could imagine that after weeks and months it was a feeling that would get to you and begin to undermine your morals and your judgment.

He gestured me to a chair across from his desk and sat. When I was sitting too he laid both fists on his desk and stared at them, like he was deciding whether to keep them or not.

"Dr. Bassett," he said suddenly, "we are preparing a nuclear strike against Israel."

I frowned and nodded. "I had gathered that much."

He shook his head. "No, you don't understand. You are not here to assist with that strike. You are here to assist in building an arsenal with which to deter retaliation. The rockets we will use to strike Israel are already built and functional."

I felt my skin turn cold and the room seemed to rock. He was watching me carefully. I forced a smile and arched an eyebrow. "Built and functional?"

"Standing by. The nuclear warheads have already been fitted. We are waiting for word from Tehran."

My mouth had gone dry. "Wow," I said, and forced myself not to lick my lips. "You are well ahead of what Western governments believe." I paused, trying hard to organize my thoughts. "And you actually plan to strike?"

He smiled, and for the first time I saw something wicked in his eyes.

"It's a bit different when it becomes real, isn't it? One

thing is some indefinite point in the future. Quite another is tomorrow, the day after, perhaps even today."

"So soon?"

"Does that change things?"

I shook my head. "No, it doesn't change a thing. It just redefines my job quite a bit, doesn't it?"

He sat back and laced his fingers across his belly. "I'm afraid it does not wash the blood from your hands. You, as the head of the rocketry department, will naturally be required to launch the rockets."

"Yes," I said blankly, trying desperately to think. "I guess that makes sense. I hadn't thought about that."

"So," he said suddenly. "What *is* the plan, and what do we want from you? The plan is to strike at Israel probably within the next seven days. Not even I know the exact date. I will be informed at the appropriate time, and then it will be merely a question of a couple of hours, just the time necessary to make ready, feed in the coordinates and launch. I will give you the launch codes, and you will take it from there."

I frowned and shook my head. "What about the Iron Dome system? It has so far taken out almost ninety percent of the missiles and mortars directed against Israel. And we're talking about small rockets a few feet long. One solitary IRBM of the size you need for a nuclear warhead capable of taking out Israel completely? It will never get through."

His smile was complacent. "The Iron Dome's radar detects incoming at about seventy kilometers away. That's about forty-five miles. From detection, in a few seconds, it calculates the trajectory and decides whether it is going to hit a populated area. On the basis of that data, a *person* makes a decision whether to intercept or not.

"If he decides to intercept he fires a ten-foot-long Tamir Interceptor, which travels at almost two thousand miles per hour, guided by ground-based radar, toward the target. *Once in range*, its own sensors take over and it locks on to the incoming and delivers a thirty-five-pound warhead which destroys the enemy missile."

He shrugged and spread his hands wide. "This is highly sophisticated technology combined with highly skilled, well-trained Israeli troops. But, at the end of the day, Dr. Bassett, it all depends on one thing."

I shook my head again. "What?"

He smiled. "Radar."

I arched an eyebrow. "You plan to take out their radar first?"

"Oh no, no no. That would be far too difficult. You see, your late predecessor, Dr. Bassett, was an expert in stealth technology, and what he designed for us was a stealth rocket." He gave a short laugh. "It is like nothing you have ever seen. It looks more like a spaceship than a missile. I believe they are bringing one into the lab to work on its guidance system. You will see it later."

He leaned back in his chair and raised his right hand like a Nazi salute.

"It will soar high into the stratosphere for about ten or fifteen minutes. It will reach the apex of its trajectory, and then start to plunge toward Tel Aviv at about fifteen thousand miles per hour. And—" He sat forward and smiled broadly. "When it is over Jordan, Hezbollah and Hamas will begin a steady barrage of rockets from Lebanon. In seconds the Iron Dome will be taxed to the limit, and they will never even see the...," he paused and grinned, then said with great deliberation, "*three* stealth missiles hurtling at them out of the sky—not until it is far too late. Israel will be annihilated."

"But..." I struggled for a moment. "Jordan, Syria, Palestine, Saudi, Egypt...," I leaned forward for emphasis, "*Jerusalem and the Dome of the Rock*, for crying out loud! You will not only destroy the most sacred places in Islam, you will slaughter millions of Muslims!"

"Yes." He nodded for a long time, then gave a small, one-sided shrug. "Most of them will be Sunni. But this is what must be done. It is the will of Allah and it will announce the end of the Great Shaitan, and the beginning of the Kingdom of God." He arched an eyebrow and regarded me for a long moment. "Can you cope with this, Dr. Bassett?"

"Of course I can. Nothing has changed. It's just momentous news, and a lot to take in."

"American presidents like to talk about the New World Order. This will indeed be a New World Order. The balance of power will shift drastically. Iran will rise and Islam will be the great power now. You will find that if you serve Allah, Dr. Bassett, he can be a very generous master."

"I have no doubt."

"Go," he said suddenly. "Go to your rooms. Get some rest. After lunch I will introduce you to your team of engineers and you will see the blueprints that your predecessor was working on. You will also have your first look at the Atar missiles." He smiled again. "I am sure you will be keen to get to work."

"Yes," I said, and meant it. I laughed. "Though I confess I am a little disappointed."

"Oh?"

"That it will not be my rocket that changes the world order. Professional pride." I stood. "Thank you for the tour and for all your help, Mr. Abdul. I'll see you later."

I stepped out of his office and headed back through the long, empty corridors toward my rooms, wondering what the hell I was going to do. Time was not just desperately short, it was running out as fast as a damned Atar rocket screaming out of the sky to annihilate ten million people in an apocalyptic flash of fire and radiation.

And as far as I could see there was absolutely nothing that I could do to stop it.

FOURTEEN

Gallin drove west along the coast toward Ramsar, with the blackness of the Caspian Sea on her right, and the blacker mass of the mountains on her left. Her instinct screamed at her to floor the pedal and make the Turkish border in five hours. But her training took control, turning her into an ice-cold machine. A woman with no veil, with no covering on her hair, driving a BMW registered to a man, did not stand a chance in hell if she was stopped for speeding. She had to stay cool, drive within the speed limit and make steady progress.

She glanced at the fuel gauge. She would need gas at some point shortly after midnight. That would be a problem. A woman pumping gas alone at night in Iran was bad enough. At one in the morning it would have consequences.

Sparse suburban areas separated by semi-rural patches of fields slipped by in a slow, steady pulse of light and dark inside the cab. A dilapidated, decaying stretch of sidewalks and beachfront cafés on her right was partially illuminated by ugly, aluminum lampposts. Some cast a dull, depressing light. Others flickered intermittently, allowing the shadows of the beach to crawl in and encroach on the slowly dying suburbia.

Suburbia, she thought, with a twist of irony, needs prosperity and decadence to flourish.

Finally, after slightly more than an hour, at the beach resort of Kelachay, the road began to veer away from the coast and climb gently through fertile fields which were quickly enveloped in blackness, as the coast towns fell behind her. To her left now the massive black forms of the Elburz Mountains began to grow closer, silhouetted against a moonless sky.

But it was not for another hour, when she came at last to the small village of Punel, that the road turned finally sharp west and began to climb steeply into the dense mountain forests. Soon all she could see were the cones of light cast ahead of her by the headlamps sweeping back and forth at every bend in the road, playing across the huge walls of towering pines. She climbed for another hour and found herself eventually in a broad clearing where the road ran straight for maybe half a mile through a cluster of buildings. Some were houses, dark and sleeping, others were more like barns. Then, on the left of the road, in a large pool of desolate light, she saw a gas station.

The decision had to be immediate. Once she came out of the mountains everything would become more difficult. The remoteness was her ally right now, but once she was out of the mountains the towns would be bigger and the access to the police and other authorities would be faster and easier. If she was going to buy gas, it had to be now.

The thoughts flashed through her mind in less than a second and before she knew it she was stepping on the brake, spinning the wheel and pulling off the blacktop into the gas station forecourt.

She pulled up by the pumps, pulled the scarf over her head and climbed out of the car. She knew she was going to have to pay cash, and she knew that could be a problem because she'd have to enter the shop, but she told herself she'd cross that bridge when she came to it.

She shoved the nozzle in the tank and something, a movement, a small noise, made her turn and look toward the shop. There were three guys. One was the gas station attendant. He was standing with his hands in his pockets looking at her and smiling. It wasn't a friendly smile. Behind him there were two more guys. They were leaning against the doorjamb with their arms crossed, grinning like they were getting ready to have a good time.

She turned away and tried to ignore them. After a time the flow of gas stopped and she shoved the nozzle back in its housing on the pump. Then she moved, as demurely as she knew how, keeping her eyes on the ground, toward the shop to pay for the gas. When she came to the door the attendant, a young man perhaps in his mid-twenties, blocked her path. She looked up into his face and spoke quietly.

"I need to pay for the gas."

"Why don't you tell me," he said with a grin that suggested he had an IQ in double digits, "what a cute girl like you is doing out all alone in the mountains at night?"

One of the boys at the door, wearing jeans and a vinyl jacket, said, "Yeah, tell him."

"My father is ill and I need to find a doctor."

He turned to his pals, laughing. "Her father is ill and she needs a doctor!"

"Please, let me pay and leave."

The third guy, wearing a pencil moustache that looked like it belonged to his older brother, said, "She wants to pay, Sully. Tell her what the payment is."

And suddenly the situation felt ugly. The laughter had gone from their faces. She glanced around and saw the security cameras.

"OK," she said quietly. "I'll do whatever you want, but away from the cameras. It could be bad for me, and also for you. Let's go behind the shop."

He looked back at his pals. They all laughed, but it was an ugly, nervous laugh. "OK, boys," he said like a punk from a bad, '50s B-movie. "Let's go."

She walked a couple of paces ahead of them, removing the long shawl from her hair. She heard soft grunts of laughter from behind her. She turned the corner into the dark, took a few paces and turned to wait for them. The attendant was the first. He stepped toward her. She smiled and moved in close to him. Still smiling, she looped the shawl around his neck and smashed her knee into his crotch. She took a quick step back as she doubled up, pulled down hard on the shawl and smashed her knee into his face. The whole thing took less than two seconds. As he went down his two pals were gaping. The whole fabric of their reality was disintegrating in front of their eyes.

Gallin helped that disintegration along a little by delivering a crushing side kick to the side of the leather jacket's knee, and she enjoyed the satisfying crunch and crack it made. He opened his mouth to scream. She didn't need that, so she crashed her elbow into his open jaw and he crumbled into a broken mess on the ground. That left the pencil moustache who was staring at her gaping, still unable to process what was happening.

She winked at him. He frowned and she ruptured his liver with a devastating front kick.

She broke the other boys' necks, put the shawl back over her head and covered her face, then entered the shop. She went behind the counter and found the office. There she destroyed the security cameras' recording unit, pulling out the DVD. Then she returned to the shop, popped the DVD in the microwave, emptied the till, grabbed a handful of sandwiches and a couple of bottles of water from the fridge, and returned quietly to the car. She thought about setting fire to the place but decided against it.

She pulled out of the gas station and started her descent out of the mountains, toward Khalkhal, the Ardabil province and Turkey. She ate as she drove. The sandwiches were surprisingly good and she realized how hungry she had been.

As she ate she started to think. Until now she had been on automatic pilot, with her thoughts occupied with how she was going to get enough gas to make the border. Now she had solved that problem, she was practically out of the mountains and had about three hundred miles to go, and six or seven hours of darkness left. Things had improved, even if just a little.

Her plan now was to get to Urmia, aiming to cross the border at Serow. Before getting there she would have to leave the road, dump the car, lose herself in the mountains and slip into Turkey somewhere south of the border crossing. From there she would call her father and get him to arrange her extraction. That was now her plan.

———

BACK IN CHALUS the cops were scouring the city, searching the beaches and raiding the cheapest, seediest hotels. Wherever she had gone to ground, they were certain she had no way of leaving town. She had no ID and no money, and no change of clothes. It was a matter of simple logic that sooner or later somebody would notice a woman wearing a man's military trousers and shirt.

While these raids were being carried out, Fatima Gholami sat and watched television, glancing occasionally at the clock on the wall, wondering if her husband would come home that night. She hoped he wouldn't. Since he had started going with prostitutes and drinking illegally, his breath had started to smell. She had also noticed that it was increasingly difficult for him to perform. And when that happened he got angry with her and beat her. But if he found his satisfaction with a prostitute, usually he just came home late and went to sleep.

At twelve o'clock, at about the time that Gallin was breaking the gas station attendant's neck, Fatima switched off her TV, went to brush her teeth, climbed into bed and drifted into a contented sleep. She was not a very imaginative woman, but she had a strange intuition that in the next day or so she was going to receive some very good news. It was just a feeling she had.

———

AND AS FATIMA GHOLAMI slipped down into deep, dark sleep, Aila Gallin slipped down the dark, winding road through towering, dark pine trees, into the Khalkhal valley. At about one AM the trees began to thin and soon she saw a radiant moon high above the western horizon. She entered the valley, crossed the small, sleeping city of Khalkhal and left it on the Khalkhal-Hashjin Road, pushing ever farther west. She drove on through the small hours without rest but also without incident, daring, as two o'clock turned to three, to feel very cautiously optimistic.

She skirted the vastness of Lake Urmia on her right, its depleted waters reflecting only a dim glimmer of moon. She then skirted the city of Urmia, keeping to Valfajr Street in the suburbs, her eyes glued to her mirrors as much as to the road. Her gamble was that any police patrols would be in the center of town, and the suburbs would be largely ignored. Whether her theory was right or not, she made it through town and soon passed the university on her right, and left the lights of the city behind her. Shortly after that she passed the small town of Rajan, sleeping among dim, twinkling lights, and the Silvana Lake Nature Reserve. And suddenly she was aware that she was barely thirty miles from the Turkish border.

A hot rush of adrenalin in her gut brought also the realization that she was closing in on death. From here on in she was not just hiding in the dark. This was where her gamble either paid off or she was shot. It also brought home to her a fact she had been carefully ignoring since she had stolen the car. And that was that on the Turkish side of the border she was only going to be marginally safer than in Iran. Israeli-Turkish relations were at an all-time low, and the increasing radicalization of Islamic feeling among the Turkish people, fueled by President Erdoğan's rhetoric of hate, meant that Jews in general were not Turkey's favorite people. So her chances of landing in prison as a Jewish spy on the far side of the border, if she was stopped by the cops, were only marginally less than on this side.

Her one, main advantage was that she could move around the streets without having to dress like a nun, and she would not be stopped by the cops for not covering her hair.

Lights up ahead told her she was coming to an intersection with route sixteen, which would carry her to the border, just six miles away. She knew it was time to dump the warmth, safety and speed of the car. The next part of her journey would have to be on foot, and might well be the most difficult and the most dangerous part so far.

She killed the lights, pulled off the road into an area of rough, sparse scrubland where a dirt track wound in among two large hills, found a spot where the car would not be seen from the road, and killed the engine.

When she climbed out of the car she was struck by the cold air. She told herself that cold was going to be her companion and her friend for the next few hours, keeping her awake and alive. She made herself an improvised ruck-sack out of her shawl, and stuffed in it a couple of remaining sandwiches from the gas station, two bottles of water and two semiautomatics from the cop shop. She also slipped the slob's cell into her back pocket, then made her way back to the road. Everything was very still and very silent, and she knew that dawn was only a couple of hours away, three at the most, and by the time the sun came up in the east, she had to be deep into the Hakkari Mountains that ran either side of the border.

She sprinted across the road and scrambled down a bank to a small river, across which she could see a broad area of farmland, and, beyond the fields, a welcome area of forest. She waded into the river and found it was deeper and colder than she had expected. Waist deep in the freezing current, she had to hold her improvised rucksack above her head until she could drag herself out on the other side. Being wet in the intense cold was not helpful. So she slung the rucksack across her back and set off along the track that skirted the field at a steady jog, making for the woodland which she could now see, by the faint light of the dying moon, sprawled up into the foothills of the mountains.

She reached the tree line after a couple of minutes. From what she could make out they were mainly small, gnarled oaks, but they offered cover and the air beneath them was not so cold. Steadily the ground began to rise. She was exhausted from lack of sleep and soon her legs and her back began to ache. She badly needed rest, and above all sleep. But it was imperative that she make the border before the sun began to rise. If the cops—or worse, military intelligence— had put together her escape with the murder of the slob on the beach and the disappearance of his BMW, the morning could bring border patrols, dogs and helicopters. It would also alert the Turkish authorities that an Israeli spy was attempting to cross into Turkey. Which would mean more patrols, dogs and choppers on the Turkish side. It was a situation that was not an option.

She had to keep going and keep climbing. So she kept her eyes down and watched her feet step and push, step and push, through the damp moss and leaves, climbing ever higher through the trees.

FIFTEEN

The address was on Holland Avenue, in the Bronx, not far from the railway lines and the zoo. Neither Aunt Peg nor Sarah was familiar with the Bronx. The few times they had come to New York it had been to Manhattan, in a coach to see the sights. The sights had not included the poorer, marginalized parts of the Bronx.

They came off the Bruckner Expressway and onto the Boulevard at White Plaines and turned north. They followed it under the Westchester Avenue railway bridge and over the Cross Bronx Expressway. It seemed at first to be an area of broad, leafy streets and pleasant residential homes.

But a second bridge that carried them over the railway lines carried them into territory that was subtly changed. The broad streets were not flanked by pretty suburban houses, but by anonymous apartment blocks. The front yards and the trees were fewer, and the light from the street-lamps seemed duller, and more inclined to create shadows for hiding in rather than light. Dilapidated shops crowded together with graffiti-covered roller blinds. By the time they turned left into Rhinelander Avenue, all Aunt Peg could see about her was a desolation of dilapidated buildings, shop fronts with names written in Arabic script, and what people there were were all men—either young and dressed in hoodies or older dressed in Muslim clothes.

Panic gripped at her heart.

"If we get out of the car here we'll be mobbed and killed." She gripped her niece's arm. "For God's sake let's get out of here and go home!"

"Aunt Peg! Will you please stop! I don't know what's come over you. Honestly! Since we left Lebanon you have been..." She searched for a word but couldn't find it and instead said, "Here it is."

She pulled in to the left and parked outside a two-storey clapboard house that had been painted a strange kind of ochre-beige. Sarah and Aunt Peg sat staring at each other for a moment. Aunt Peg shook her head.

"This is a really bad idea."

For just a second Sarah looked worried, then she sighed. "Oh, Aunt Peg, you shouldn't buy into all that negative propaganda. Come on, Ali and his family are really sweet, spiritual people. Let's just give them the gift and then we can be on our way."

Aunt Peg sighed, and with a deep sense of misgiving she climbed out of the car. Sarah opened the trunk and from one of the bags she extracted the gift-wrapped box. From the far corner, by the steps of a small church, three young men in hoods watched them.

"Please hurry, Sarah."

Sarah slammed the trunk closed and they both

approached the door. There was a small, plastic bell which Sarah pressed twice. Inside a door closed. A moment later feet tramped down the stairs. The door opened a couple of inches and a dark, bearded face with dark eyes peered out at them.

"Yes?"

Sarah spoke anxiously, smiling. "Raza? I'm Sarah, Ali's friend. We've brought you a present from Suleiman, your father in…"

The man was putting his finger to his lips, saying "Sh! Sh! Sh!" He unhooked the catch and yanked open the door. "Give me!" He reached for the package, but Sarah backed up a step, frowning.

"Well, hang on. Are you Raza? Ali was very specific I had to deliver it only to Raza, personally."

The man stepped forward, reaching for the box. "Yes, I am Raza. Give me."

Aunt Peg blurted, "For God's sake give it to him and let's get out of here!"

"Give me the box!"

Sarah was scowling and put the box behind her back. "I don't believe you're Raza! How do I know you're Raza?"

"I am Raza! Give the box!"

She was backing up and he was going after her, trying to reach behind her back. Aunt Peg's fingers were at her mouth. "Oh my god!" She repeated it over and over like a mantra. "Oh my god! Oh my God, just give him the damned box!"

"This has great spiritual significance…"

The man suddenly roared, "*Stupid bitch! You give me the box!*"

Feet were tramping on the stairs inside the house. Shadows wavered through the door and two young men in jeans and T-shirts emerged. Sarah and the man who claimed to be Raza were struggling over the box. Aunt Peg had started to scream.

"For God's sake, Sarah! Give him the box!"

Now the two newcomers descended on Sarah, grabbed her and Raza snatched the box from her fingers. For a weird moment they all stared at each other, motionless. Then Raza said something. It was a split second. Then one man was suddenly dragging Sarah toward the house and the other grabbed Aunt Peg by the hair and started pulling her after Sarah. She screamed for help. Sarah was screaming and kicking. Raza slapped her hard across the face. She gasped and her legs went to jelly. Then the sirens started.

To Sarah they seemed to come from everywhere. The world tipped and reeled around her, and seemed to be filled with wailing, howling noises and screaming voices.

To Aunt Peg it also seemed they came from all sides. And wherever she looked she saw unmarked cars hurtling toward her. And men, running, shouting. She felt pain, excruciating pain in her head, as she was dragged, stumbling by her hair toward the house. She knew that she must not go to the house. She knew that if she entered the house she would die. She heard her own voice, shrill, hysterical, screaming, *"Stop! Stop!"* But there were other voices, men's voices, bellowing, also shouting, *"Stop! Freeze! Let them go! Stop! Now!"*

The she saw. She saw, suddenly in slow motion, how Sarah was being dragged along the sidewalk. She struggled and scrabbled trying to stand. She saw how the man who was dragging her pulled a very black gun from behind his back. Then, weirdly, the wall seemed to spit. Small beige and pink shards of wood and brick erupted in plumes from the wall. For a timeless moment they seemed to hang, suspended in the air.

Then there was a hard ugly *smack!* And the man who was dragging her gave a small whiplash and his head exploded in a shower of red and black gore. She fell to the sidewalk and crawled against a car, unable even to scream, her heart pounding too fast for her to breathe.

Across the sidewalk she saw the man dragging Sarah point his gun down. She was paralyzed by disbelief. The gun jumped and spat fire, and Sarah's head seemed to jump, then flop. Then he staggered back as six, seven, eight bullets smacked into his body. The third man yelled something, there was a dry *crack!* and he folded to the ground. Then there was an immense, impenetrable silence. Beyond it feet ran and voices shouted, but they could not penetrate the absoluteness of the numb silence that existed inside her.

Then arms encircled her, held her tight and moved her away, away from death, away from blood and ugliness, away from Sarah.

That was when she screamed and collapsed, calling for her niece, calling on God to make it not true, begging for the madness not to be true.

They took her to Federal Plaza, up to the 23rd floor, and gave her coffee. Shortly after that a medic came to see her and asked her if she wanted to be sedated. She didn't know if she wanted to be sedated or not, but thought of her father and asked for a shot of bourbon. He hesitated and said he'd see what he could do.

Five minutes later a man in his fifties in a gray suit came in holding two paper cups. He smiled at her and winked. It was a kind, paternal sort of a wink.

"Your coffee," he said, and handed her a generous shot of whiskey. "I'll have to wait a few hours for mine." He sat. "Agent Harris, you can call me Joe if you like. Everybody else does. Mind if I call you Peggy?"

She shook her head and felt an irrational rush of gratitude that made tears well in her eyes. "Peg," she said, and quickly sipped her drink.

"Peg. Been a rough couple of weeks, huh?"

"You could say that." She gave a tearful laugh. "I had no idea, till…" She frowned, struggling to think. "Till we were going to the airport. Then I just started to get the feeling something was wrong. And it wasn't till we were driving into the Bronx that I realized she'd been talking to Ali on her computer for I don't know how long!"

"Ali?"

"In Lebanon. Beirut. I couldn't work out at the time why anyone would want to go there on holiday. But she convinced me. And now she's…"

Her lower lip curled in and she started to sob. He handed her his handkerchief. She took it and for a while all she could say was, "I can't believe she's gone. She's not here…"

Agent Harris waited until the spasms had passed. Then he asked her, "Do you know what was in the parcel?"

"He said it was a small, gold amulet that had belonged to his cousin's great, great-grandfather or something. It was given him by some holy man, Ali ibn something Talib. I remember Talib because it reminded me of the Taliban. He said it was inscribed with the sacred words of the prophet. I suppose he meant Mohammed."

Agent Harris nodded. From his pocket he pulled a plastic bag. Inside it there was what looked like a large, steel battery with two wires protruding from the bottom. He studied her face as she frowned at it. "Do you know what this is?"

"No." She shook her head. "It looks like a piece of plumbing."

"This is what you carried across the border, believing it was a gold amulet inscribed by Imam Ali ibn Abu Talib with the sacred words of Mohammed. Maybe you weren't so far wrong at that. This is a detonator for a strategic nuclear device."

She gasped audibly and covered her mouth. "But Sarah couldn't have known!" Then her eyes bulged as she realized the implications. "I didn't know! I suspected something but not *this!*" She pointed at the device. "And I told the cops at the airport..."

He smiled. "Peg, nobody suspects you of complicity. If you hadn't spoken to the agents at JFK, we might not have found it. But this," he held up the detonator, "this is not enough. If there is a detonator, we have to assume there is a bomb. Where?"

She shook her head, her eyes still wide. "I don't know."

"Do you think Sarah might have known?"

"I don't know what to think anymore."

"I can imagine, Peg. But you know what would be really helpful? We need her cell phone and we need her computer, and we need to go through her apartment and her possessions with a fine-toothed comb. If we are lucky her conversations with Ali might tell us something. And we can save a lot of time if you authorize us to do that right now." He held up the detonator again. "We may have bought some time with this. But we don't know how many they sent, or where they came in."

Weeping, biting her lip and repeating her niece's name over and over, she signed the papers he put before her. And fifteen minutes later, fifty miles away in Bridgeport, Connecticut, eight patrol cars from the Bridgeport PD raced through the city streets with their sirens wailing. Four headed for Sarah's apartment, and four headed for Aunt Peg's house. By morning not a square inch of either dwelling would be unexamined. In particular, Sarah's tablet, desktop PC and laptop would have been flown to the New York field office on Broadway, and the most intimate details of her life would have been scrutinized.

Right then, Agent Harris, having dispatched digital copies of the signed documents to the Bridgeport PD and the local FBI Office on Lafayette Boulevard, along with instructions to raid the two dwellings, re-entered his office and hunkered down in front of Aunt Peg.

"We have a car waiting," he said. "We're going to take you home now."

———

MEANWHILE, six thousand miles away, in Tehran, General Muhammad Zaidi cradled the telephone he had just hung up and sat staring at his bare feet in the dark bedroom. Ali in Beirut had failed. The Mossad would now be alerted by the Pentagon, and they would go after Ali. He glanced at his clock. The green, luminous numbers told him it was five thirty AM. He picked up the telephone and dialed a number. It answered after the second ring. The general said, "Raza is dead. The American bitch is dead, but her aunt is with the FBI."

"Ali?"

"May Allah grant him seventy-two virgins, despite his incompetence."

"I understand. I will make a call."

In Beirut, Lebanon, it was four o'clock. Ali was asleep in his room. He didn't hear the telephone ring in the next room. He didn't hear Zegham Abbas sit up and take the call. And he didn't hear, three minutes later, his bedroom door open. Zegham, who was like a brother to him, stood with tears in his eyes and whispered, "*Alahu Akbar, 'akhi.*"

The suppressed shots made little noise beyond a *phut!* The fist struck Ali in the temple, the other four punched into his chest, ripping through his heart and his lungs. He died instantly, and took the secrets of the strategic nuclear device, concealed in the dense woodlands along the Hudson River, with him into the dark night of his death.

Next day a Mossad katsa charged with the surveillance of Ali's apartment reported that a carpet had been removed from the place and dumped in the back of a van, and he suspected Ali was in the carpet. A hastily assembled team followed the van, guided by an equally hastily scrambled drone, which tailed the van for thirteen miles south along the coast to Khiam al Damour, where it turned inland and followed the Damour Beit Ed Dine Road, winding twenty miles into the mountains to the wilderness of the Barouk Natural Reserve.

There the men were filmed bundling the body out of the van and dragging it in among the undergrowth. It was as Zegham Abbas and his two companions were climbing back into the van that the Mossad team closed in. They took out Zegham's companions swiftly and efficiently, bundled Zegham into the trunk of their car and headed at speed toward the border at Metula, just thirty miles away. There he was transferred to an official vehicle and driven, again at speed, a hundred and ten miles to the Mossad headquarters in Tel Aviv. There he was taken directly to an interrogation room where he was handcuffed to a chair which was bolted to the floor. His interrogators knew well that torture was both ineffectual and unreliable as a means of acquiring intelligence. But they also knew that time was running short and they had a potential holocaust on their hands; and this man had to be made to talk, and talk soon. Precious minutes and precious seconds were draining away.

Colonel Benjamin Gordon entered the interrogation room and pulled a chair up just inches from Zegham Abbas.

"We know you and Ali sent a detonator to New York using two American women as mules."

Zegham spat elaborately on the floor.

"Were other detonators sent?"

"Why don't you ask your mother? That Jewish whore sleeps with Arab studs."

Gordon nodded to a guard at the door who stepped out of the room. Then Gordon leaned close to Zegham and spoke quietly to him again.

"Listen very carefully to me. I know where your mother, Fazia, lives, and I know your sister Habiba, who married just a year ago, has a baby boy. I know where they live too."

Zegham went pale and began to expostulate. Gordon shook his head and said, "No, listen to me. A doctor will come into this interrogation room in a moment and he will inject you with a serum perfected by the Russians during the Cold War. It is called SP 117. When you are injected with this, it is impossible to resist telling me the truth. Nobody can resist.

"Now, when we have what we want, we will give you the antidote. And the thing about the antidote is that it makes you forget everything. You will remember nothing. We will hold you a week, give you some very convincing bruises." He shrugged. "If you prefer we can kill you. It's your choice. But nobody will ever know that you talked. Not even you. And your mother and your sister and her baby will all be safe. We will say we got the information from Raza, in New York."

The door opened and Zegham stared at the doctor with tears in his eyes.

SIXTEEN

I STOOD IN MY SMALL CELL-LIKE ROOM WITH MY head reeling. I had never actually experienced panic, but I figured this must be pretty much what it was like. My brain was trying so hard to outrun time, trying to analyze all the problems I had to deal with in the next thirty seconds, all I could think of was nothing: a big, blank void in my head. There were no solutions. It was out of my hands and it was just too late. Gallin was dead and I was alone and unarmed in a military facility that might have five hundred soldiers in it for all I knew, where three nuclear missiles were, in that very moment, being trained on Israel for the dual purpose of annihilating the Jews as a nation, and creating a new, Islamic World Order.

I had to do something, but there was nothing, realistically, that I could do.

I don't know where it came from. It was a memory, something I had heard once, long ago, from a crazy Norwegian shortly before he died. I remembered that when he finally went down he had fifty-four rounds in him, and he had killed twenty-seven Columbian cocaine traffickers.

We had been sitting in a bar late at night, drinking tequila. The next day we were flying out from Mexico to Medellin. He knew he was going to die. He told me so. But it didn't seem to worry him. He'd said to me, "Remember, Alex Mason, there is always a better choice than cowardice, if you have business to take care of." Then he laughed and shook his head. "One day, long ago, my life was shaped and my fate was fixed. Fearlessness is better than a faint heart for any man who puts his nose out of doors. The length of my life and the day of my death were fated long ago. But *how* I live, and *how* I die, that is my choice."

With no clear idea of what I was going to do, I pulled my leather bag from my wardrobe, extracted my cell from the lead-lined compartment, shoved it in my pocket and stepped out into the passage again. I had fixed certain landmarks in my mind when Mr. Abdul had given me the grand tour, and I found my way back to the large, steel elevators that descended to the rocketry labs, where the engineers were still at work.

I stepped out of the elevator into the vast hangar-like room and stood looking around for a moment. There were about a dozen men in blue overalls, some of them wearing yellow hard hats. There were machines and workstations which were beyond my comprehension, and among them large sections of a very exotic-looking rocket. It looked like some kind of a hybrid between a very advanced stealth jet and a UFO. Several men were gathered around it working on its innards.

There were also, against the walls, long benches with a

huge variety of computer hardware. Several men sat there, hunched over monitors. Those guys were dressed in white coats and had no hats.

I noticed a guy approaching me. He had a clipboard, a white coat and a yellow hard hat. He also had "Chief Engineer" stenciled on his brow. He held out his hand and smiled.

"Dr. Bassett. We were not introduced earlier. I am Samy Gupta, the chief engineer. It will be an honor to be working with you. How can I help you? We were told you would be starting work tomorrow."

I smiled blandly. "Yeah, I was told that too. But I was curious and restless and thought I'd come and have another look around."

"Oh, excellent. That is very good. Anything in particular...?"

I didn't want to be too obvious, but neither did I have a lot of time to waste. I pointed to the rocket they were working on. The nosecone was open and there were two guys working on the electronics. Just beyond them I could see a large platform that suggested a hydraulic lift.

"Put me in the picture, Samy. I think for the next few weeks I am going to be depending on you quite a bit." We both laughed like that was funny and started to walk toward the rocket. "What are you guys doing here?"

He gave me a long explanation that included a lot of words like "vector," "parabolic arc," "vernier thrusters" and "gimbals." He also told me they had played with the idea of differential thrusters and throttle engines, but discarded the idea in view of the Soviet experience.

I nodded a lot, like I knew exactly what he was talking

about, and pointed over at what I was now fairly convinced were hydraulic lifts.

"This feed the arsenal or the silos?"

He led the way and I kept pace while he explained.

"This particular one feeds the three silos. There are actually twelve silos, but only three are active at the moment." He laughed. "One thing is digging a hole in a mountain, quite another is equipping it as a silo for a nuclear missile!"

"Tell me about it!" I laughed in a "been there done *that!*" sort of way. "So the lift carries the rocket up..."

"Forty feet. The rocket is then picked up by a crane which is controlled by the MCS over there..."

He pointed at the long bench of computers I had seen earlier.

"The MCS...?"

"Missile Control Station. The missile is then placed upright on a hydraulic platform and raised into the silo. It would be a lot easier to feed the silo from above, but secrecy is everything at this stage."

"It sure is. Presumably the silos are camouflaged above..."

"Oh, goodness yes! They have the sliding, retractable lids, irregularly shaped and painted with sand-textured paint. Impossible to spot from above."

An insane idea was forming in my head. I asked, it in an off-hand manner, like I was ticking off boxes for the sake of completeness, "And retraction is an automatic part of the launch protocol, I presume?"

Samy danced his head from side to side. "Well, Mr. Abdul had demanded an automatic, integrated launch procedure by which we would trigger the launch, and all the stages, including the opening of the silo hatches, would follow automatically. However, Dr. Benini...um, your predecessor, incorporated a series of overrides because he claimed he did not trust automated systems. So, as of now, the silos open automatically on launch, but the override safety measure exists."

I frowned at him. "I would say that was quite important. Wouldn't you? I don't want to think what would happen if one of those hatches failed to open."

He gave a nervous little laugh. "That would be very bad news. But all the stages can be manually overridden from the MCS."

I nodded toward the MCS. "Show me."

We spent the next hour going over the launch protocols and guidance systems, which Samy explained to me, "Are pretty much nonexistent. Once the target data and the launch codes are fed into the onboard targeting unit, the missile is by and large an autonomous vehicle."

"So in-flight sabotage is practically impossible."

He shook his head. "Impossible. Unless they shoot it down, there is no way of stopping it. It will go to its target and it will detonate."

I grinned malevolently. "And of course, thanks to this exceptional design, the rocket is invisible to radar."

He nodded. "It will drop out of the sky like a bolt from a vengeful god. There will be time only to make peace with one's creator, if one is quick."

"Oh, brave new world, that has such weapons in it."

He grinned. "*The Tempest.*"

"Misquoted. You work around the clock?"

"Until now we have had no chief scientist, so we have

done little more than maintenance. The rockets are made and armed, so we only need to maintain them and await launch instructions. So, we work till about six o'clock and then we knock off for the night."

"Splendid, Samy. Well, I can assure you that as of tomorrow you will have plenty to do. We are going to make the best damned rockets on the planet."

He grinned broadly. "Oh, very motivating."

"Say," I smiled benignly, "it's about lunchtime. Why don't you boys finish up here and take the rest of the day off. I'll hang around and look things over. But I want everyone here on site at six sharp in the AM. How does that sound to you?"

"Oh, that's splendid. Yes, splendid, indeed."

He toddled off and talked to the boys while I strode around with my hands behind my back trying to look like I knew what I was looking at. After about fifteen minutes they began to leave in twos and three, until Samy was the last one left. He came and saluted me and said he'd be there at five thirty the next morning.

I watched him go to the elevator and, as the doors slid open and he stepped in, Dr. Borg Ericson stepped out. He showed me his pipe in a kind of bookish salutation and strolled across the room, looking around as he went.

"I bumped into Mr. Abdul. He was on his way to see you. I told him I would show you around and take you to lunch. Odd, to see the place so empty and silent."

"I'm giving them the afternoon off. Their work is done. Tomorrow I'll start working them hard on the next generation of rockets."

"Did you clear it with Abdul? He doesn't like breaks in routine."

"Nope."

He smiled. "No doubt you'll have a visit from him soon. He is watching us, you know. He or his security team." He glanced up at the ceiling.

I laughed. "Did he send you to warn me?"

"No." He smiled. "Show me the warhead." We walked over to the gaping cone of the missile and he leaned in. "The radiation, though slight, disrupts the listening devices. Your venerable predecessor told me that."

I stared at him a moment. "And why would you want to disrupt a listening device? Are you starting a trade union?"

"Not at all. I am just curious. You are not a rocket engineer. That is patently obvious. So who are you?"

I scowled. "I should be offended."

"But you're not. You clearly haven't the faintest idea what is going on. You don't know a booster from a cone. So what's the story?"

"Has Abdul got this impression too? Am I going to be shot in the morning?"

"No, he's far too stupid. Your secret is quite safe. Whatever it is."

"Well, I'm grateful, Dr. Erickson, but you have completely misread my..."

He frowned and interrupted me. "Why don't you use differential thrusters on this design, with throttled engines, instead of gimbals?"

I arched an eyebrow at him and said, with as much conviction as I could muster, "After what happened to the Soviet rockets?"

He removed his pipe from his mouth and regarded me for a moment. "And what *did* happen to the Soviet rockets, Dr. Bassett?"

He had me. Even if I had recovered, and recovered well, I had taken too long to answer.

He looked back into the rocket. "Dr. Hirsch and Dr. Henley are relatively new additions to the team. They have been here just six months. They are interested in nothing but their work. Dr. Schneider has been here for years. He is the father of the project and believes in it, ideologically. Pierre and I have been here a year, and we do not believe we will ever leave. We believe it was no accident that your predecessor died exactly when his part of the program was finished."

Quietly, deep inside, I swore in ways that would make a sailor blush, and away in the District of Columbia my parents spun in their graves. I affected the gestures of a sincere scientist discussing his work with an esteemed colleague, for the benefit of the cameras, and asked, "Why are you telling me this?"

He pointed at a circuit and gestured toward the tailfins.

"Because I do not believe you are a rocket engineer, and once that premise is accepted, the reasons for your presence here become a very narrow spectrum."

"Like what?"

"Sabotage, by one of a small number of agencies."

"That's ridiculous."

He laughed. "No, it isn't. It is eminently possible. Pierre and I were blackmailed into this program. Naturally neither of us believe in it. But there is very little we can do. Look what happened to poor Enzo."

"So assuming your crazy idea were correct. So what?"

He walked to the tail of the rocket and gestured at the three nozzles. "If the theory is correct," he said, looking me square in the eye, "the three exit together."

Cute. "You're out of your mind."

He put the pipe in his mouth, still gazing blandly at the nozzles, and shook his head. "That is very unlikely." He shrugged. "And if you give it a few seconds' thought you will see that it must be a collaborative endeavor."

"What guarantees do I have that Abdul didn't send you to test me?"

"The same that you have right now, and that you had before. None. The same that I have, or Pierre." He began to walk toward the MCS, pacing slowly. I fell in beside him and he gestured again with his pipe. "But, do you really think they want to embark on another search? They are satisfied they have found the man for the job. That is all they care about. I, on the other hand, think you are here for a purpose. And when you leave, we want to go with you. The cooperative strategy offers you far more options than you had before." He gave a slightly bewildered laugh. "Though I confess I have no idea what you think you are going to do."

"How did you know I was going to be here?"

"Pure chance. I was on my way to your room and I saw all the technicians leaving early. I asked them where they were going and they told me you were here and had given them the afternoon off. Which rather confirmed my suspicions."

What he was saying made sense, and my instinct told me to trust the guy. Besides which, I was clean out of time to test theories. I had the ball and I had to run with it, and if he turned coat on me I'd just have to break his neck. I figured I'd give him a little surprise and see how he reacted.

I smiled and glanced at my watch. "Erickson, you are trying to lure me into a trap, but it's not going to work. I am here to do my job and get paid. Listen, you figure Abdul is in the common room or the bar by now?"

"Probably. Why?"

"Let's go grab a drink with him. I need to ask him some questions. We'll drop by TV central on the way."

He frowned at me as we stepped into the elevator. "TV central... Oh, you mean..."

"You know where that is?"

"Yes. Fourth floor. By the way, I used to box in Denmark. I was regional champion in Fyn."

I looked at him, sighed and shook my head. Whether he was telling the truth or not, pretty soon I was going to have to offload him. Especially if the French guy decided to join up, they were going to slow me down big time. And I needed to get out of Iran and over to Tel Aviv fast.

The doors slid open and we stepped out into a broad, concrete corridor with matte, cream walls. Other corridors branched off it. Dr. Erickson turned right, muttering, "These are the dormitories for the workers and the soldiers. We estimate two or three hundred of them. Why they feel they need so many, I am not sure. But they are here and they are well trained. The TV central, as you call it, is just here. I don't know how many men there are..."

We came to a sage green door and I rapped hard with my knuckles. Erickson said, "What are you doing?" The door opened and there was a large soldier scowling at me. He began to ask something, but I bent my left knee, flicked my left hip and drove my left fist deep into his liver. It was a death blow.

As he went down I slipped my arms under his armpits and carried him forward a few steps into the control room. I heard Erickson splutter, "*Satan's ossa!*" I ignored him and cursed softly as I saw four more soldiers looking up at me with round eyes and sagging mouths. Dr. Erickson closed the door as I said frantically, "Help this man! Help him! He has collapsed!"

Erickson translated hastily into faltering Farsi as I let the dying man drop, and slipped his Glock from his holster as he went down. The first two shots were easy. The third was getting to his feet and the fourth had his weapon trained on me, ready to fire when Erickson brought his right arm up savagely into the soldier's wrist. The gun went off. I felt the round breathe hot air over my head and I shot him in the heart.

Erickson moved to the screens and started to scrutinize them. I was wondering what the hell my next move was. I saw a clipboard hanging on the back of the door and figured it was the shift rosters. I checked them and said, "We have five hours left of these guys' shift. That means five hours before they're found."

He seemed not to hear me. "These are the silos," he said. "There are two groups of twelve soldiers there. I don't know how you plan to..."

"Don't worry about it. Listen to me. Now I am committed, I need to know. Why are you doing this?"

"I told you. Pierre and I fear for our lives. We were brought to the program by blackmail, and we had no idea that it would culminate in this. We cannot be party to the annihilation of an entire people."

Did I believe him? I didn't know, but I hadn't much choice, either. I asked him, "Where's your pal, Pierre?"

"In his room. Here." He pointed at a screen.

"And Abdul?"

"Still in his office."

I thought for a second, then sighed.

"OK, listen to me. You go get your pal. I'm going back to the lab. Pretty soon all hell is going to break loose. That's your chance to get out. It's the best I can do."

He stared hard into my face, understanding my meaning. He faltered, hesitated, then said, "We will wait till the last moment for you."

I nodded. "OK. Go."

SEVENTEEN

I DIDN'T RETURN TO THE LAB. I TOOK ONE OF THE guards' Glocks, slipped it in my waistband behind my back and made my way quickly to the elevator. I slipped my pass into the keypad and keyed the ninth floor, where Abdul's office was. The doors slid open and I walked quickly to his door and knocked.

"Come!"

I pushed open the door and stepped in. He frowned up at me but made an effort to smile. The message was he was being tolerant.

"Dr. Bassett. How can I help you?"

I went and leaned on his desk. "The launch codes for the missiles. I need them."

His frown deepened. "No, you don't seem to have understood, Doctor. Not until we receive instructions from Tehran…"

The right cross caught him hard on the cheekbone and sent him and his chair spinning. A seasoned fighter would have shrugged it off, but Mr. Abdul was an administrator, and the toughest fight he'd ever had was getting the cap off a pen. I walked around the desk and pulled the chair off him. He was grunting and trying to stop the floor from moving. I rolled him on his back and pressed the muzzle of the Glock against his chest.

"I think you are the one who does not understand, Abdul. I want the launch codes, and I want them now."

"You are insane. I can't..."

"I haven't got a lot of time. I have more questions I need to ask you, and I haven't got time to persuade you. So I will start putting bullets through your joints every time you give me the wrong answer. Do I need to do that?"

"No! No, no..." He glanced at the security camera in the corner, probably thinking he had a whole platoon charging to his rescue, if he could just fob me off for a while.

"They're all dead," I told him. "All five of them." I showed him the Glock. "That's where I got this. So where are the codes?"

He swallowed hard. "In my head."

"Good. Get up." I dragged him to his feet. "We are going to go down to the lab now, and we are going to launch the three missiles against Israel. You understand? Now let me explain something. I am desperate, and nothing is more dangerous than a desperate man. You double cross me, call for help, lie to me—you do anything I have not told you to do, and I will put a bullet through your spine and into your intestines. That is the slowest, most painful death known to man. Are we communicating clearly?"

He nodded, and the pallor of his skin said he had understood.

I shoved him out the door and walked beside him to the elevator, with the Glock stuck in his back under his jacket. We traveled down in the elevator to the basement where the rocketry labs were located and the doors slid open. I propelled him across the floor to the MCS and when we got there I kicked him in the back of the knee and snarled, "Lie facedown, don't move and don't make a noise."

He lay with his hands over his head and his eyes squeezed tight, while I rattled at the keyboard the way Samy had shown me, and manually overrode the hatches. I locked them so that they would not open on launch. Then I turned to Abdul. I rolled him on his back, knelt on his chest and pressed the muzzle of the Glock on his right knee.

"Bullshit me and I will blow your knee in half."

"No, please, anything, anything you want to know. I cooperate."

"English woman, Jewish, arrested as a spy."

He nodded desperately. "Yes. I told you."

"Where was she taken?"

"I will tell you everything I know. Please don't shoot me."

"Start talking."

"They take her to Chalus..."

"*Where?*"

"Chalus, please, on Caspian Sea. She is taken to amoni—amino...anoni, anonymous police station for interrogation by senior officer." He was sweating profusely and trembling violently. I didn't figure he was in any state to be making it up.

"Were they going to keep her there?"

"Yes, I don't know, maybe not, I think so, but probably interrogate her and kill her. Or trade her."

I was thinking hard and fast. "OK," I snarled, "the codes."

"But—"

"What?"

"She escapes."

"*What?*"

"She escapes. Don't kill me. You see I am helping. She escapes. She kills interrogator and escapes."

That made sense. "Where to?"

"Nobody knows." He frowned a face of incomprehension. "You are going to kill her? You want to kill all the Jews? We are already doing this..."

"Yeah, but I'm in a hurry. The codes."

He talked me through the launch process of each missile, entering the code for each one at the beginning and the end of each sequence, when all three were live I pressed the big, ugly red button, there was a distant roar and the ground shook violently under our feet. I shot Abdul through the head, took his wallet and his cell and ran. The roaring and rumbling was growing louder and the walls were beginning to shake. The doors slid open on the main entrance floor and I staggered out of the elevator. There were people running and swarming everywhere. The walls and the ceiling of the cave were splitting and cracking open. The one thing I was uncertain of was whether the exploding rockets would be sufficient to drive the plutonium together in the warheads and trigger a reaction. I had doubted it, but by the intensity of the explosions I was beginning to wonder. I searched around for a buggy. In the melee I saw a couple speed past, but couldn't reach them.

Then there was the blaring of a horn and the screaming of people and tires. I looked to my left, toward the exit, and saw a Land Rover hurtling toward me. I pulled the Glock from behind my back and took aim. The horn blared again and the driver's door opened. It was Dr. Pierre Blanchet.

"You drive!" he shouted.

A couple of soldiers were scrambling for the truck. I shot them and climbed in. Erickson was in the passenger seat. He smiled placidly and said, "Hello."

I rammed the truck in reverse and floored the pedal. There were sickening bumps, knocks and crunches. I tried not to think about them. A couple of shots whistled past or pinged off the chassis. That seemed like a good time to turn her round. So I hit the brake and spun the wheel and found myself face-to-face with a steel door twenty foot high and forty foot across.

Pierre said, "I go," and with that he was out of the truck and running toward the guard hut beside the door. The walls were still shaking and the vanguard of the panicking crowd was catching on us, overwhelming Pierre as he reached the door of the hut. A moment later the door started to roll open, and at the same time the truck was surrounded by people scrambling and hammering to get in. I hammered down the locks and saw Pierre emerge from the hut and start battling his way toward us. I rammed the truck in reverse, floored the pedal and heard people scream, saw them scatter. I put it in first and roared forward, scattering more people. Erickson lowered his window and hollered to Pierre, "*Take my hands! Take my hands!*"

Pierre ran and jumped, gripping on to his friend, who gripped his arms and hooked his elbows over the door. Other hands clawed at him. I floored the pedal again, slammed in second and third. Shots rang out and we stormed through the door. Third, fourth and fifth and we were hurtling out through the narrow entrance to the complex, along the long, straight blacktop, away from the nuclear facility.

Erickson was shouting at me, "*Stop! Stop! I can't hold on!*"

I slammed on the brakes. We skidded to a halt. Pierre fell, staggered to his feet, wrenched open the back door and clambered in. Then fell across the back seat as we took off and hurtled away along the road, putting the miles between us.

Then the ground trembled. The whole desert trembled. In spite of myself I came to a stop on the road and we climbed out. The whole mountain shuddered and the narrow pass seemed to come loose and crumble. There was an almighty detonation, followed by two more in rapid succession and the roof of the mountain exploded toward the sky in a vast, terrifying cloud of dust and rock that rose in billows and impenetrable folds toward the sky, blocking out the sun.

I heard Erickson's voice saying, "It is radioactive. We have to get out of here. Come! Go! Go!"

We clambered back in the truck and started the winding drive back down the mountain toward the village of Dash-tak. Behind us the sky was turning black, obscured with smoke and dirt. We didn't stop at the village, but sped through it blaring the horn for the gaping villagers to get out of the way. As we emerged from the town I said to Erickson, "Pierre didn't get out to look at the explosion."

He stared at me a moment, then turned in his seat to look in the back.

"He is dying," he said matter-of-factly. "He is shot, bleeding from his chest. He will die."

I shook my head. "We'll go to the airbase. Get a chopper to take him to the nearest hospital. Nobody knows what happened except us."

"The authorities will interrogate us, and him if he recovers. Sooner or later one of us will crack."

"We have Iraq to the west, the whole of Iran to the east, Armenia, Azerbaijan and Turkey to the north. And a dying man in the back seat. What do you suggest?"

"I don't know. But we cannot leave him in an Iranian hospital."

We didn't talk for a few minutes. I knew there was truth in what he was saying, but I was damned if I could think of an alternative.

We hit the flat farmland outside Abarj and topped a hundred on the long straight road heading for the Shiraz airbase. It was as we were approaching Jafarabad that the two choppers appeared and thundered overhead, hurtling toward the towering column of dust that was blocking out the northeastern sky.

Moments later a column of Jeeps and trucks hurtled around the bend up ahead. I pulled off the road and the lead vehicles tore past us in a fog of sand and dust. I counted fifteen vehicles before two jeeps pulled up and a colonel and a captain climbed down and approached us. Overhead two more choppers thundered toward the smoldering, erupting ruin of the nuclear base.

I lowered the window, holding the plastic ID card Mr. Abdul had given me.

"*We are scientists!*" I shouted above the roar of engines. "*The silos exploded! We have an injured man. Dr. Pierre Blanchet! He urgently needs a hospital!*"

The captain said something to the colonel, then turned to me. "*Are there other survivors? Is there radioactivity?*"

"*There is total chaos up there. I am sure there are survivors, lots of people badly injured. The mountain collapsed in on the silos. I am pretty sure there is no radiation.*"

He translated this to the colonel as two airbase ambulances went howling past. I added, "*Dr. Blanchet is crucial to the program. We must get him to a hospital!*"

He translated that too. The colonel nodded and made a phone call. The captain turned to us and leaned on the window.

"Go to the base. A helicopter will be waiting for you. It will take you to the Emam Sajad hospital in Yasuj."

I saluted him and as the last of the column rolled by I took off again, burning rubber across the farmland and the hills. When we pulled up at the airbase there was a paramedic team ready. As we jumped down they wrenched open the rear door and lifted Pierre out onto a gurney. Then they ran and we ran with them, through the base, which was practically empty, and out onto the tarmac where a chopper was waiting with its rotors thudding.

They lifted him in and fitted a drip in his arm. The young medic in charge then waved both hands at me in a negative motion.

"You go! We must stay. Many injured. Go!"

I gave him the thumbs up and as they backed away toward the buildings the chopper rose into the air, angled north and sped away across the ochre desert. On our right we could see the massive, black column of toxic, radioactive smoke still folding itself up, in enormous billows, into the atmosphere.

I turned and looked at Erickson. He was holding Pierre's wrist. He met my eye and gave a small shake of his head. "He's gone."

I rose and moved into the copilot's seat. The pilot glanced at me and frowned. I said, "Do you speak English?"

"Little. You no be here. Go back."

He jerked at the rear with his thumb. I shook my head. "No. Listen." Looking out the window I could see he was following the road north. I said, "You land." I pointed down. "Go down. You get out. I fly." I made the motion of flying the chopper.

He scowled and said, "No! You go back!"

I sighed and pulled the Glock from behind my back, aimed it at him and pointed down at the road.

"Go down."

He made the mistake of reaching for his sidearm. I shot him through the temple, unfastened his harness, reached across him, opened his door and shoved him out with my feet. Then I clambered into his seat and strapped myself in as the chopper began to yaw and twist out of control. In the back I could hear Erickson losing his cool and swearing in Danish. It seemed to have a lot to do with Satan and his bones.

I ignored him and slammed the cockpit door closed

again. Erickson struggled into the seat next to me and stared at me for a long moment. He pulled his pipe from his pocket and put it in his mouth, shifting his attention to the desert ahead. After a moment he said, "You are descending. Do you know how to fly a helicopter? Do you know you are descending?"

"We need to get below the radar, or they'll start asking us who we are."

He went silent again, then said, "Good. Tell me again you are just a rocket scientist."

I smiled. "I don't know about Denmark, Börg, but rocket science is a tough game in the States."

He didn't laugh. He sighed and sat and watched the endless desert skimming below us. After a while he asked, "So what is the plan now?"

I nodded. "I am glad you asked me that, I was wondering the same thing. We have all of Iran on our right, Iraq and the Persian Gulf on our left, and Armenia, Azerbaijan and Turkey ahead of us in the north." I paused, thinking about my last conversation with Abdul. "And I have another problem," I added.

"It's not enough? You have more? What other problem?"

"I need to go and find a lady."

EIGHTEEN

IN THE BRONX, THE MAN WHO IN LONDON HAD been Ahmed, and had threatened to kill Aaron for his incompetence, sat behind the wheel of a GMC Yukon six-liter V8. Beside him was Agent Harris. Agent Harris knew the man as Colonel Paul Cohen.

"The local PD have been told to stand by and we have instructions from the director to let your boys comb the place before we move in. Whatever forensics we have are at your disposal. They're listed in the report. Should be on your desk by now." He shrugged, still feeling a little bewildered. In all his years in law enforcement he had never seen anything like it. Usually it was the cops stepping aside to let the Feds move in. He had never seen the Feds asked to step aside for a foreign agency, not even the Mossad. Till now. "Pretty much all we've done is secure the area," he said.

Colonel Cohen nodded. "Good. We're grateful to you for the courtesy, believe me. I know it's irregular, but we'll hand it back to you the way we found it, when we're done. When my team arrives send them in. I'll be inside."

He swung down from the cab, pulled a small rucksack from the back and entered the house. He had a small team of three agents who were on their way, but he had made a point of arriving ahead of them. He first checked that the house was empty and then ascended the stairs to the top bedroom, which he knew from their collaboration with the Bureau had been occupied by Raza. Once there he pulled on a pair of latex gloves and opened his rucksack. From it he extracted a six-page document printed in Farsi, which he dropped in a drawer in Raza's desk. Then he descended the stairs at a trot and began to inspect the kitchen, meticulously bagging mugs, cups and cutlery for prints and DNA. Presently one of his team would find the report upstairs. He felt a warm glow of excitement at the thought, but he controlled it. He did not show it.

Outside, Agent Harris was on the phone to the director.

"Yes, sir, Colonel Paul Cohen, of the Mossad. He's in the house right now. His team's on their way. Sir, how come they get to conduct this investigation here in New York? This is our jurisdiction..."

His superior's voice cut him short. "Because it's a courtesy, Harris. You know what that is? It means when our counterterrorism boys need to conduct unofficial investigations in Israel, they politely look the other way. Don't worry about it. Nobody is going to know, and you will get all the credit." He sighed heavily and seemed to relent a little. "Harris, we're talking about a tactical nuclear device, and the intelligence we're getting is that this might be a feint. That the real target is Tel Aviv, or Jerusalem. These guys know what they're doing, so we're cooperating and giving them some latitude."

Agent Harris felt oddly sick. "Yes sir," he said, and watched a dark Audi SUV pull up. Two men and a woman climbed out. They looked cool and professional. They suited up in white plastic without talking to anybody, and went inside the house.

———

JUST OUTSIDE TEL AVIV, not far from the Glilot-Ma'arav Interchange, Aaron sat in a windowless office in the vast, concrete maze that is the Mossad headquarters. He was bruised, inside and out, and deeply scared, too. Across the desk from him was a man who looked average in every way. He was in his early fifties, fit, lean, gray-haired and blue-eyed. He was Colonel Benjamin Baker, and he was one of the most dangerous men in Israel. Aaron knew that that made him very dangerous indeed. When he spoke his voice was pleasant and quiet.

"You want to explain to me what happened, Aaron?"

"Alex Mason is a senior agent with ODIN, in the USA..."

"I know that."

"He has worked with Alia a couple of times and it seems they became close."

Colonel Baker nodded several times at his desk. "I know that too, Aaron. I am waiting for you to tell me something I don't know."

"He wanted to talk to me about what had happened the night Aila was killed—"

"Abducted."

"Yes, I'm sorry. Abducted. We presume—"

"Don't presume. Unless you know something the rest of us don't. Do you know something the rest of us don't know, Aaron?"

"No! No, not at all, sir."

"So how did you wind up on Tayo beach, with seven bails of crap beaten out of you, and tied up with your own bootlaces?"

Aaron swallowed hard. "After I'd spoken to him in the morning, I had the impression he was not going to drop his personal, private investigation. Her disappearance is a confidential matter, so I thought I had better meet with him somewhere private and..." He faltered.

"Kill him?"

"No sir! I would not hurt an ally."

"He hurt you."

"Yes sir."

"And Marion and Joseph."

"Yes, sir."

"Why? What made him do that, Aaron? This is one of ODIN's best agents, a close friend of Israel. I am trying to understand what makes a professional agent of his stature beat up three Mossad operatives."

Aaron closed his eyes. He was cornered and had no way out. So he told the least damaging of the lies available to him.

"We tried to scare him off."

Colonel Baker made a temple of his fingers and stared at it for a long time with no particular expression on his face. Finally he said, "You tried to scare him off."

"Yes, Colonel."

"You—the three of you—took the confidentiality of the investigation into Aila's disappearance very seriously."

"Yes, sir."

"Do you often beat up allied agents who take an interest in the welfare of Mossad agents?"

"No, sir."

"No, sir..." He raised his eyes and skewered Aaron with them. "So what made this case so special?"

There was a tap at the door. The colonel's face tightened with irritation. He snapped, "Come!" and the door opened. A young man in a suit handed him half a dozen pages clipped together. They were in Farsi. He said, "This through from New York. The director wants you to read it. Then he wants you in his office for an emergency meeting in fifteen minutes or less."

The young man left and closed the door. Colonel Baker turned back to Aaron and narrowed his eyes.

"You have two options, Aaron, two paths you can go by. You can tell me the truth, or you can lie. If you lie I will catch you out and you will pay very dearly for it. Or you can tell me the truth—the whole truth—in which case things will go easier for you. But caution." He raised a finger. "If you choose to tell me the truth, just make sure you do it before Marion and Joseph do. Otherwise it will have no value at all. Wait for me here. Do not leave my office."

The colonel rose and left the office, reading, as he walked, the report that had been sent through by Colonel Paul Cohen from the New York field office. As he read it, his blood turned cold.

———

And six hundred and sixty-six miles to the north and east, several hours earlier, Gallin had sat shivering violently under an oak tree, watching the horizon turn a revolting mix of powder blue and pink, and wondering whether she had crossed yet into Turkey. She had no point of reference, except that roughly fifty yards above here there was a sharp ridge, and somehow she had come to assume that beyond that ridge she would be out of Iran and into Turkey. Her legs hurt badly, she was exhausted and deeply sleepy. Her entire body cried out to her for rest, to take just a few minutes to sleep.

But she knew well what that could mean, and being spotted and caught just fifty paces from the border was something she was not prepared to allow. She forced herself to her feet and pushed, one step after another, up the steep incline, grabbing at shrubs and branches to pull herself up. One thing and one thing only dominated her thoughts. One thought filled her mind. She must reach the top of the crest before the sun came over the horizon, and allow herself to slide down the other side, well out of reach of any Iranian patrol.

The ridge was narrow, barely fifteen feet across. Concrete posts had been sunk into the ground fifteen or twenty feet apart, and barbed wire had been attached to the posts to a height of some twelve feet. She took the scarf, now empty of provisions, tore it in half and wrapped the two halves around her hands. Then planting her feet either side of a post, she scaled the wire, keeping her body well clear of the wire. When she had reached the top, leaning on the post with her hands, she swung one leg over, then the other, and jumped.

She lay, bruised and exhausted, on the Turkish soil as the sun, molten orange, welled over the edge of the world in the east, beyond the cruel wire, and the sky turned a pale gray-blue. After five minutes, she rolled on her belly and stared at the sight below. There was a road that ran left to right, some three hundred feet below her. Beyond that, perhaps four hundred yards away, was what seemed to be a quarry of some sort. Right now it was empty of people or activity. To her left there was more quarry, and to the right, she knew, was the border post, maybe five hundred yards away.

One thing was clear to her. Both the quarry and the border post meant there was a town nearby. She scrambled forward and slid and tumbled her way down the steep slope of dust and stones until she hit the bottom in a painful, bruised, grazed mess. There she lay on her back, staring up at the gradually dawning sky.

But still she did not sleep. She forced herself to sit and pulled the slob's phone from her pocket. She dithered a moment, unsure whether to call her father or the HQ in Tel Aviv. She was aware she was using an unsecured line, and both Turkey and Iran could be monitoring calls to Mossad numbers.

On an impulse she re-enabled the phone's GPS, recalled Mason's private number and sent him her location on What-sApp. She gave it thirty seconds, then disabled the GPS again and switched off the phone. Then she began the longest mile of her life, wending through the lifeless, dry, dusty quarry until she came eventually to the scattered buildings of the small village of Esendere, on the Turkish side of the border.

By the time she got there the streets were just starting to come to life. Roller blinds rattled across the golden morning, men and women stood winding down their awnings with long poles, casting long shadows against gold and pink walls; and from within the terraced cafés, red and silver Gaggia machines screamed and the smell of early morning cigarettes wafted out, blended with the rich smell of coffee.

Hunger twisted her belly. All the currency she had in her pockets was Iranian, and to change it into Turkish lira she would have to show some ID. She figured, looking the way she did, trying to change Iranian currency with no ID, it might take all of five minutes for her to land in a Turkish jail.

A wave of fatigue and depression washed through her. She could see the map of the Middle East in her mind. She had three routes back to Israel: She could cross all of Turkey and then get a boat across the Mediterranean, she could cross Iraq and then Jordan, or she could cross Syria. And right then all three were impossible.

She stood on a street corner, staring across the road at a shopping mall that was not yet open. Inside it was an international currency exchange that was also not yet open, and which she could not use anyway, because she had no ID. She needed a viable, executable plan. The plan was, she told herself, get some Iranian lira, get a car, drive six or seven hundred miles to Samandag on the Mediterranean coast and sail to Israel.

It was a bad plan, but the hunger and the exhaustion were making it hard to think. She retraced her steps to the last café she had passed. It had a few tables out on the side-walk and the owner was standing in the doorway, smoking. She smiled at him. He took in her clothes and her hair and decided not to return the smile.

"Do you speak English?"

He shrugged, pulled down the corners of his mouth. "Little."

She pointed toward the shopping mall. "The money exchange is closed. Can I get some breakfast with *rials*?"

He shrugged again and looked away. "Is more expensive. I have trouble. I must exchange."

"How much?"

In the end he charged her forty bucks for two cups of coffee and a toasted roll. She paid happily, ate, drank and thought.

What she really needed was a phone, preferably a burner. She also needed to get to a town where the main point of focus for every damned person in the town was *not* the Iranian border. If she could satisfy those two criteria, she was confident she could get home to Israel or London within twenty-four hours.

It was true that she had sent Mason her location less than two hours previously. She had no reason to assume he hadn't received the message, and he was probably right then taking steps to come and get her. But then, if she could get a burner, she could call him and talk to him.

That made her smile.

Across the road, a couple of hundred yards away, she saw the mall doors open to the public, and after a while the first couple of cars pulled into the parking lot. She stood, went to what passed for a lavatory in the café, washed her face and hands and ran her fingers through her hair. The result wasn't fantastic, but it was better.

She left the café and, in the growing warmth of the morning, crossed the road and headed for the shopping mall parking lot. By the time she got there, there were eleven cars scattered randomly near the entrance. About half of them were less than two years old. They were no use to her. Of the remaining six, four were less than five years old and they were no use to her either. She focused on the other two: a beaten-up Fiat Panda and a Toyota pickup that was at least twenty years old. That was the one.

Unconsciously she formed a mental image of the owner and what departments of the store he'd be in. She went inside and it didn't take her long to find him.

There was only a handful of people wandering the aisles. The café was just opening and most of the shops were still closed. But the big supermarket, BIM, was open. Gallin grabbed a small cart and went in. She figured the chances were high that Turkish men, especially those driving Toyota pickups, did not go grocery shopping unless both their mother and their wife were dead. So if this guy was in the supermarket at this time of the morning it was because he was buying something his mother or his wife could not be trusted to buy themselves. That would put the item in the hardware or automotive departments.

She found him buying coolant for his truck. He was weather-beaten and leathery, somewhere between forty and a hundred, with hard calloused hands, a humorless face and a rollup hanging from the corner of his mouth. She congratulated herself on being a smart cookie and had a look at a rack of windshield wipers. She sighed and shook her head like she couldn't find the ones she needed, just in case anyone was watching, and left by the "no purchase" exit to make her way back out to the parking lot.

She waited for him at the back of his truck, leaning on a lamppost. She let him pop the hood and refill his radiator before she approached him. He met her smile with a face that said she probably needed whipping for no particular reason other than she was a woman.

She ignored the expression and asked him, "Do you speak English?"

He shook his head, slammed the hood and pushed past her. She turned with him, still smiling. "Do you speak Glock?" she said, and thrust the cannon into his gut. He froze and swallowed. She led him around to the passenger side, opened the door and shoved him in. Then she slid in beside him, pushing him behind the wheel, and said "Go," indicating with the weapon that he should shift.

He shrugged. "*Nered?*" he asked, which she gathered meant, "Where?"

She pointed to the road, in the opposite direction from the border post. "That way, genius. But just make sure you turn left at Albacoikee."

She grinned. He nodded. He'd understood the gesture, if not the words. He fired up the engine and pulled out of the lot. Step one of part one of phase one of her plan, was in motion.

NINETEEN

Colonel Benjamin Baker entered the chief's corner office. The chief was standing at his window looking out across the freeway at Yuntzman Park, away toward Hapirza Gap Beach, half a mile distant. The colonel dropped the report on the chief's desk and the chief turned to look at him. He was a powerful man, not tall but strong, seasoned in combat and experienced in undercover work. He was not a man who was easily scared, but the gray pallor of his face and the shadows under his eyes spoke now of a very deep fear.

"Sit, Benjamin, tell me about this report. What does it mean?"

"Cohen is a good agent. He has years of experience. He is loyal. His integrity is beyond question."

"I am not questioning his integrity, or the veracity of the document. I am asking you what it means. Have a whisky. It may be the last chance we get."

Colonel Baker sat while the chief poured them two generous measures of his twenty-five year-old Laphroaig.

"We suspected Captain Aila Gallin had been murdered," he said as the chief handed him his drink. "Ariel told us as much."

"Poor Ariel. His daughter was everything to him."

"Has he seen this?"

The chief shook his large head. "I will telephone to him later."

"The Iranian state police were notified by an anonymous source that she—a female Mossad agent posing as a rocket scientist—was attempting to infiltrate Iran's nuclear program. She was detected..." He paused and closed his eyes. "She should never have attempted such a thing. I told Ariel..."

"We both told him, Benjamin. But she was determined. She knew the risk. They both did. Go on, talk me through it. But I want some analysis, Ben. I need you to tell me what this *means*."

Colonel Baker took a moment, drew breath. "She was detected. The report does not state where the information came from. It is hard to believe we have a leak..." But even as he was saying it he was thinking of Aaron, whom he had just left in his office. "But equally hard to believe she was careless!" he said, savagely. "Sir, have two men go to my office and bring Aaron Goldman here! Alert security to stop him from leaving the building!"

"Are you insane?"

"Do it, man!"

The chief picked up his phone and gave the orders. Colonel Baker was on his feet, striding the room. "How could I have..." He turned savagely on his superior and pointed at him. "He was in London! He was on Ariel's team. He was Aila's backup the night she was killed!"

The chief scowled and shook his head. "But Aaron has proved himself again and again. He is a loyal agent. It makes no sense."

Colonel Baker cut across his superior, his eyes darting across the tiled floor as though pursuing thoughts that were running wild there.

"He claimed he lost Aila's trail for about forty minutes the night she died. In that time he informed Aila's contact, a Lebanese or an Iranian called Ahmed, that Aila was Mossad."

"How can you possibly know? Why would he do that?"

"I don't know," Baker growled. "Money? Personal reasons? The point is he is the *only* one who could have informed them. And that very night they took her."

The chief was frowning, shaking his head. "Why snatch her in London? Why not wait for her to go to Iran and arrest her there?"

Colonel Baker stared at his chief, his mind racing. "I don't know," he said at last. "But the fact is that this report confirms she was taken to Iran, interrogated and executed."

"It doesn't make sense. Why risk being caught by MI5...?"

"If she was taken to the embassy, and then embarked with diplomatic personnel, there would be little risk. The crucial point is, sir, that the report confirms that she was right, that they have weapons-grade uranium and their rocketry program is well advanced." He held up two fingers in a V. "There are two things we must consider here. First is that the girl who was killed in the raid in the Bronx was transporting a nuclear detonator. The FBI and Cohen both confirm this independently. The second is that in this report Hezbollah is put on alert to begin a deluge of rockets on Israel that will tax the Iron Dome to its limit, so that their IRBMs with nuclear warheads can get through."

"I can't believe it! Jerusalem is as sacred to them as it is to us! Besides, millions of Arabs would die."

"Most of them Sunni," Colonel Baker snarled. "The Shi'ite and the Sunni hate each other almost as much as they hate us. Don't look for logic in their thinking, sir. If they could wipe Israel off the face of the Earth and decimate the Sunni population into the bargain, the destruction of the temple would be a small price to pay in their minds. Kaaba, in Mecca, is their most holy site."

"I can't believe it," the chief said again.

"We have to face it, sir." Colonel Baker leaned across the desk, staring down at his chief. "We have known from the beginning that Iran was an existential threat to Israel. The bomb in the Bronx, like the rockets from Hezbollah, are distractions. The report makes that clear. The *real* attack is a nuclear strike on Israel, and it could be weeks, days or hours away. We *cannot* delay. We *must act!*"

There was a tap at the door and two plainclothes agents looked in. They were frowning, confused. Colonel Baker snapped, "Well?"

"It's Aaron Goldman, sir. He's dead."

"*Dead?* I just left him in my—"

"In your office, sir, yes. That's where he is. He put his gun in his mouth and blew his own head off."

"Jesus!" Colonel Baker swore softly under his breath.

The chief reached for his telephone. "Deal with it, Benjamin. I am going to call the prime minister."

————

IN THE BRONX COHEN rang Aaron for the third time. For the third time he got no reply. He tried Marion and when a voice he did not know came on and asked, "Who is this, please?" he hung up and for a few seconds his gut burned with panic. He dared not call Joseph.

He was at the south end of Soundview Park, walking by the Bronx River. He pulled the SIM card from his cell, cut it in four with his Swiss Army knife and scattered the pieces into the dark water. Then he wiped all trace of his prints from the phone and hurled that into the water too.

It was the end. He knew it was the end. But if it would just play out the way it should, if the timing were right and he could pull it off, he would give his life gladly. He stood looking out at the sun, fractured on the East River, like a million tiny souls in a vast, dark universe. He said a silent prayer for all God's warriors who had fallen over the millennia to bring his people back home to Israel, to Jerusalem. He begged God's forgiveness if he had failed, or if he had strayed from the path, and begged Yahweh to ensure Israel's ultimate victory over her enemies.

Then he turned and walked back toward the Bronx River Avenue, where he had left his car.

TWENTY

ERICKSON DIDN'T ANSWER STRAIGHT AWAY. HE watched the arid terrain a few hundred feet below us hurtling past for a while before saying, "You need to go and find a lady."

It wasn't exactly a question. It was more like he was presenting something absurd for me to look at.

I nodded. "Yeah. She's a friend. She was arrested as a spy by the Iranian secret police."

"Is this...?"

"The one who was going to replace Dr. Benini, yeah."

He muttered something about Satan's bones again, gazed out of his side window and asked, "So where is she?"

I grinned at him and laughed the brief laugh of those who know that nobody else is going to find something funny. "I don't know," I said.

"So..." He raised his eyebrows.

I cut him short and said, "On the map. Find me Chalus, on the Caspian Sea."

He took a map from beside the copilot's seat and opened it, talking with his pipe clenched between his teeth.

"Is that where she was held?"

"Yeah. It seems she escaped."

"So you think she is lying low in Chalus? That presents many problems, Dr. Bassett..."

"No. She would not lie low waiting to be caught. That's not her at all," I said, smiling to myself. "No, if I know her at all, she has stolen a car and—" I glanced at the map. "Show me. The nearest borders are..." I reached over and pointed. He said, "Azerbaijan, Armenia and Turkey."

"No contest, Turkey. What is that, three, four hundred miles? She has stolen a car and headed for the Turkish border."

Erickson shook his head. "There are over three hundred miles of Turkish-Iranian border. How could you possibly know...?"

I cut in. "There are three crossings. Two are for vehicular traffic and one for vehicles and rail. The busiest of the three is Gürbalak-Ağn, so we can discount that. A, it's too busy and she'd run a greater risk of being stopped, and B, it's the farthest from Chalus. She'd be looking for somewhere close and quiet. What's next?"

"So, we have Razi-Kapikö, here..." He pointed and I shook my head.

"Better, but still busy. What was the third one?" I tried to remember, scouring the map with my eyes. "Serow-Esendere, there. That is the least busy of the three."

"How do you know?"

"Most important part of any plan, Dr. Erickson, is having an escape route. I checked before I came. Turkey is the easiest route to the West, and Serow-Esendere is the easiest crossing. Two gets you twenty, that is where she is."

Erickson nodded for a while. Then shook his head for a bit.

"I don't know where to begin my list of questions and objections. First of all, what are you going to do with me and, above all, Pierre? Second, how are you going to enter Turkey with a stolen, Iranian military helicopter? Third…"

"No," I said, shaking my head. "No, not at all. That is not how you do it. Think about all your problems at the same time, you might as well cut your veins and climb in the bath. You'll just be completely overwhelmed. We take one problem at a time."

"So, Pierre?"

I shook my head. "You and Pierre."

His face went pale for a moment. "How do you plan to solve us as a problem?"

"Don't worry, I very rarely throw live Scandinavians out of helicopters." He gave a laugh that was more like a wince. "I am going to call the office and get them to send an extraction team to take you and Pierre home."

"Same problem. Where?"

"At the Iraqi border, near Basra. We still have advisory troops in Basra. They could send a chopper to pick you up."

I reached for my cell but Erickson was already shaking his head.

"No, my friend. It is almost seven hundred miles from here to the border crossing. I gather your friend is Jewish?" I nodded. "Israel is as hated by Turkey as it is by Iran. If she is captured I do not want to imagine what will happen to her in a Turkish jail. To deviate your course to the Iraqi border could add an hour or two to your journey. In that time..."

He said no more but just shook his head. I knew he was right, but I also had to find a solution to the Erickson-Pierre problem.

My other alternative was to call ODIN, explain the situation and have them ask the Turkish air force not to shoot us down. And also to send some friendly officials to Esendere to receive us. The only problem was that, assuming Turkey didn't politely invite us to go to hell, it could take hours for ODIN to get through the red tape and diplomatic protocols, while the authorities quietly took Gallin off to be quietly shot. Gallin, after all, was Israel's problem, not ours.

I reached for my phone in my pocket and stared at the screen. I saw without seeing the red 1 on the green WhatsApp icon. Absently thought I would read it later, and put the phone back in my pocket.

For the next half hour we sat in silence examining every possible permutation of the very few options we had open to us. Complicating the matter was the fact that the fuel gauge told me I had barely enough fuel to get to Esendere, with zero to spare. Eventually I turned to Erickson and said, "There is only one thing we can do."

He nodded. "I know. Do it."

I sighed and reached again into my pocket for my cell.

————

SOME TWO HOURS away by speeding helicopter, but earlier that same morning, Gallin sat in the cab of a twenty-year-old Toyota truck with a Glock 17 shoved into the back of a Turkish farmer who didn't look so much scared as pissed. He kept shaking his head and muttering something guttural.

They came out of the shopping mall parking lot and Gallin indicated he should turn left. He snarled but obeyed and then rolled onto the main road that led south and west into the country, toward Yüksekova. Her plan, such as it was, she was developing as she went along. The next step was to find a quiet, secluded spot where she could pull off the road. The spot appeared about two miles out of town. There was some wooded farmland, and a broad dirt track that turned off on the far side of the road. She pointed with her left hand and said, "There!"

He muttered things that she imagined were obscenities, but spun the wheel, crossed the road and bumped and rolled along the track until a smaller path appeared on their right, which led in among the trees. She pointed again and he followed it and finally came to a halt in the midst of a small copse. They were hidden from the road and from any possible passersby.

She mimed to him to take down his pants. He looked horrified and shook his head. She placed the muzzle of the Glock on his knee and asked with her eyebrows if he would rather be kneecapped. He looked more horrified and started to undo his pants. While he was struggling with his clothes she took the keys to the truck, swung down and went round to open his door. She helped him down and told him to finish undressing. When he was done she led him deeper into the copse and, with a straight lead, put out his lights. She tied his ankles and his wrists with his bootlaces and stuffed his socks in his mouth. After that she gave him what *rials* she had and took all his Turkish currency and his driving permit, in the name of Emre Begum.

Then, after apologizing silently to the unconscious man, she climbed in the truck and rolled back onto the road. As she headed south and west again, she eased and relaxed in her seat. Now it was an hour's drive or so to Yüksekova, where she could buy a burner and call Mason. He'd have received her WhatsApp by now and she knew he'd be making arrangements to come and fetch her. But however fast he moved, he'd still be at the stage of booking flights and talking to the British and American embassies in Turkey. She figured the best thing she could do was probably get to Ankara, or at least the nearest big town with an airport.

Either way, whatever she did, she'd arrange it with Mason, and he'd get money and papers to her within a few hours. She smiled. He was a pain in the ass, but she knew she could rely on him.

Absently she looked in the rearview mirror. She saw a blue and white car approaching at speed and knew immediately it was the cops. One thing was shooting Iranian cops and rapists, but she was very clear she could not shoot law enforcement from a major NATO country. All she could do was pray to whichever deity looks out for Jewish agents fleeing from Islamic cops, to make her invisible.

She didn't become invisible. The cop car behind her pulled out to overtake and she saw there was another behind it. The first drew level with her and a cop leaned out the window, indicating to her to pull over and stop.

There was no point trying to outrun them, and she had already decided she couldn't shoot them. So her only option was to pull over and kill the engine.

One of the cars stopped ahead of her and the other stopped close behind her. One of the officers in the front car got out and came to her window. She smiled. He didn't.

She said, "Hi, is there a problem?"

"Papers."

"I have no papers."

He scowled. "You have no papers?"

"They were stolen. I am English. I am on my way to the British Embassy to collect..."

"Passport!"

"Do you speak English? Passport stolen." She mimed someone stealing a passport and added, "Embassy. British Embassy."

The cop's scowl had deepened and now he started yelling. "Get out car! Out car! Get out!"

She continued to smile and wondered about revising her policy on NATO members. "OK," she said, "getting out of car. Stay cool." She climbed down, speaking calmly as she went. "OK, Officer, I am British. I need to go to the British Embassy..."

"Who car?"

"What?"

"Who car? No you car! Who car?"

"Oh!" She gave a small laugh. "My friend, Emre, he lent it to me."

"This Emre car. I am know Emre. His car. Why you his car?"

"OK, Emre, me, keys." She mimed Emre handing her the keys. "He say, 'You take car, go British Embassy."

The backhander came out of nowhere and knocked her head back against the truck. It dazed her and made the world reel. Her overriding instinct was to kill the cop where he stood, and she had to fight hard to quell the reaction. The guy had stepped close and was screaming in her face, "*Why you car Emre?*"

He grabbed her, spun her and slammed her against Emre's Toyota. She felt the cuffs bite deep into her wrists and then she was dragged away toward the waiting patrol car. There she was shoved into the back seat and the door slammed closed. The car did a tight U-turn and they headed back toward Esendere as she sank back in her seat and closed her eyes. So close. She had come so close.

Why the hell had they arrested her anyway?

They bypassed the small village and continued as far as the border post. There they stopped outside a gray prefab, dragged her out of the car and bundled her inside. There she passed through an office where a couple of cops were typing at computers, and into a back office where a captain sat behind a desk. He had a moustache that would have made Saddam Hussein proud and looked up to regard her as they shoved her in.

The guy who had arrested her said a few words which she thought included the name Emre, and the captain nodded once and dismissed the cop. Gallin took a breath.

"Do you speak Eng…"

"Silence." He didn't shout. He just said it and continued to observe her for a moment. Then he said, "Papers."

"I have no papers."

"You must have papers."

"They were stolen."

"You must report they are stolen."

"I called my embassy. They told me to go to Ankara and they would replace them."

"You must report theft to the police."

"I apologize."

"Why were you in Emre's truck?"

"He was there when I discovered my papers had been taken."

"Where?"

She thought fast. "In the shopping mall parking lot. I discovered my purse and my passport had gone. He was very kind and offered me his truck."

"To go to Ankara?"

"No, of course not. Can I sit down?"

"No. If not to Ankara, where you were going in Emre's truck?"

"To Yüksekova."

"For what?"

The bastard was relentless. She sighed. "To collect a car rental."

"With no papers?"

She said very deliberately, "I have friends in Ankara who work at the embassy. They have arranged a car rental for me. All I have to do is collect the car and drive it to Ankara."

"And Emre's truck. We pay for Avis to deliver it back to him."

He nodded and thought about it for a moment. "OK," he said at last. "You can go."

She struggled not to look surprised. "Thank you. Now can you have..."

He interrupted her. "As soon as we find Emre, and he confirm your story."

She groaned elaborately. "But he could be anywhere!"

He raised an eyebrow at her. "Not very far if he have no car." He jerked his head at a sofa placed against the wall. "You sit. We look for Emre."

"May I make a phone call?"

"No. You sit."

She was about to sit when there was a knock on the door and it opened to reveal the two cops who had stopped her, and between them a hastily dressed and much enraged Emre Begum.

He burst through the door, wrenching free from his escort, and started screaming in shrill outrage, pointing at Gallin where she sat, advancing on the captain, hollering at him and stamping his foot as he pointed again at Gallin.

Finally the captain raised his hand and silenced the outraged farmer. He turned to Gallin. "He say you threaten him with a gun, you steal his money and you steal his truck. In his truck we find Glock semiautomatic. Who are you, what are you doing in Esendere?"

She regarded him for a long moment. "I am a British citizen, and I need to talk to the British ambassador."

He gave a small, unpleasant laugh. "Unfortunately, you have no papers to prove you are British. Right now, you are nobody. I put you in a cell and we wait. I will come and visit you sometimes. Then I think you will want to tell me everything."

He snapped some orders at the two cops. They advanced on her, grabbed her savagely by the arms and dragged her away. Captain Durmaz smiled. She was an attractive woman. He was going to have some fun with this one.

TWENTY-ONE

IN A LITTLE KNOWN OFFICE IN THE MATCAL Tower, HaKirya, in Tel Aviv, Colonel Baker sat alone at a large, highly polished oval table. He sat in a heavily padded black leather chair. The other eleven chairs, recently occupied, now stood empty. He was aware of his heart pounding in his chest. He was aware of a strange detachment in his mind, as though it had separated itself from him and was observing his panicking body from the ceiling. It was like a kind of madness. Everything was mad. It made no sense.

He was having trouble believing what he had done, what he had been a party to. And as he had looked around the room, at the other men and women in that most secret and critical of meetings of the war cabinet, he had seen the same look of disbelief, of near despair, but also that all-Israeli resolve.

They had all said it, one after the other, like a mantra. He had been the first: "We are facing an existential threat."

And they had all repeated it, first one, then another: "This is an existential threat, a threat to our very existence."

And it was true. They had the proof. This was one of those rare times in history where it is either or, fight or surrender, live or die. Exterminate or be exterminated.

The meeting had taken less than an hour. The prime minister had been there and made the final decision. The defense minister, the generals, the director of the Mossad. They had all been there. He had briefed them and in the end they had all agreed. The preferred target would be the missile silos, but they had no idea where those were. So the next preferred target must be Tehran.

And while nuclear devastation rained down on Tehran, an all-out assault would be launched on Lebanon. Lebanon must be razed to the ground so that never again might Hezbollah rise from the rubble. And only God knew where the radioactive cloud would drift, raining its poisonous fallout.

The consequences were unthinkable. But they had no choice. If they did not strike now, Iran would strike at them, and the consequences would be a thousand times worse. It would be genocide, and the rise of Iran to rule half the world.

They had gone, the generals and the ministers, to that place only they knew. The missiles were armed and being readied. And in a short while eight million people in Tehran would be vaporized, burned to death, women, children, men, Muslims and Christians alike.

And then the years of death by radiation poisoning.

He rose and left the room, knowing that he had done the only thing he could do, taken the only option available to him, yet knowing also that his immortal soul must live now in hell, for all the innocent souls he had sentenced to death.

———

IN THE IRANIAN AIR FORCE BELL 212 Mason was thundering over treetops and hilltops, driving the chopper above its top speed by the sheer power of his will. Beside him Erickson went to speak several times, but each time he glanced at Mason's face and thought better of it. A black cloud seemed to have settled on his brow that suggested questions were ill-advised.

The sun began to decline and below them shadows grew long in the golden dust. Occasionally they hurtled over a village and below them scattered villagers gazed up at them in fear and awe. Mason ignored them. He knew time was against him and his total focus had to be on arriving at the border before it was too late. Yet even as he thought that he was aware of the sun sinking toward the western horizon.

He glanced now at Erickson. "How far?"

Erickson sighed and looked at the map. He had lost track of their position long ago. But now he frowned out of his side window and saw the massive body of water, with the small city nestled on its western banks, beginning to glitter in the dusk.

"*Satan's Ossa!*" he said, "That is Lake Urmia!"

———

GALLIN HAD SPENT the whole afternoon sitting on the floor of a twelve-by-twelve cell which had recently been occupied by people who evidently couldn't control their bowels and also couldn't spell "your mother was a camel" in Farsi.

Food had been brought at lunchtime, but she had refused to eat, and had spent the time instead working through all the possible reasons Mason had not received, and probably would not receive, her WhatsApp location. She had also come to the conclusion that everybody assumed she was dead and nobody, not even Mason, was looking for her. She had realized that all of the Five Eyes nations were probably right then in an insane scramble to penetrate Iran's nuclear program, and Mason was probably in that very moment in Iran and not looking at his secure cell.

These gloomy thoughts led her to one, irresistible conclusion. The police captain who had just arrested her was now going to show up and give her a choice. Get raped or kill an allied cop. Hobson's choice.

When the two cops showed up again and stepped into the cell to take her back to the captain's office, the shadows were lying long across Esendere, and the temperature was beginning to fall. She wasn't sure how long she had been without sleep, but she figured it was around thirty-six to forty-eight hours. She was fatigued and starving and her entire body hurt.

Her cell was in a small complex of prefabs across the road from the customs office and the captain's administrative building. The cops had her arms gripped one on either side and were marching her across the dirt to the blacktop. She could feel her heart racing and her head was light and for a moment she wondered if she was going to pass out. She fought the weakness, if for no other reason than because she would rather die than show weakness to these bastards.

They dragged her across the road, pushed her through the now empty front office and into the captain's office. He looked up and smiled, and stood.

"Have you had time to think, woman?" he asked.

She nodded. "Yeah, and I am thinking this is going to become an international incident."

He stood. "Really? I don't think so. What evidence will you be able to adduce for whatever allegations you make? Besides, if you upset me too much, you might become one more stupid Western girl who dies on a stupid adventure in the wild East."

He began to unbutton his tunic.

"Besides," he said, with his voice growing thick, "things can be much easier for you. If you collaborate, you are a very beautiful woman, I can make things easier for you. I can make bureaucratic problems disappear, you know."

He hung his jacket on the back of the chair, removed his watch, laid it carefully on the desk and began to unbutton his shirt.

"This can be easy and pleasurable, or it can be painful." He smiled. "I have to tell you I enjoy both. The choice is yours."

Gallin's head was spinning in a double bind. To submit to this bastard was impossible, but to kill him was impossible too. But if she beat him or crippled him, she might as well have killed him. So defending herself was also impossible.

He took off his shirt and pranced slowly across the floor.

Gallin sneered to herself, thinking that the schmuck looked like a ballet dancer about to do a plié.

And then the thudding in her ears started again. Only this time it was louder, pounding, it seemed to her the walls were shaking, and when she looked at the shirtless dick, he was staring at the ceiling and covering his ears. He strode to the door and wrenched it open, bellowing in Turkish. She went after him and saw, directly in front of the office, great clouds of billowing dust, and within it the bent, cowering figures of the border guards backing away.

Gallin began to laugh and pushed past Captain Dick to run out of the office and into the street. There, thirty feet above the road, was the huge, thundering form of a military helicopter, pounding the air and descending upon them.

I LEANED out of the cockpit window and was surprised to see Gallin standing beside a half-naked Turkish officer, laughing and waving at me like she'd been expecting me to turn up. I settled the big, clanking bird gently in the middle of the road, let the rotors slow with a descending thud and when they had come to a halt I pushed open the door. Beside me Erickson said, "Look, I'm going to slip away. Someone's meeting me. Thanks for letting me make the call."

I gripped his hand and we shook. I told him, "Say hi for me."

"I will."

And he was gone. I clambered down from the chopper. The half-naked policeman was running toward me through the dust, waving his hands, and just behind him I could see

Gallin grinning like she'd recently been lobotomized. I ignored the naked ape and asked Gallin, "What's going on?"

"The captain was about to try and rape me."

"No kidding. It's nice to see you alive. You look like you were expecting me."

"Of course I was."

The captain finally found his voice and spluttered, "Who are you? What is this?" He gestured furiously at the helicopter. "This is a violation of Turkish airspace...! What are you doing?"

I narrowed my eyes at him a moment and said, quietly, "Shut up. Are you the commanding officer at this border post?"

"Yes! Of course!"

"Then you are about to receive a telephone call from Ankara. And I am going to need the use of your office for a while."

"Are you out of your mind?"

I took Gallin's elbow and guided her toward the office. I took in the grazes and the bruises and felt the hot glowing embers of rage in my belly. "He did this to you?"

"No, he hadn't got started yet." She was still grinning. "These are from...hell! It's a long story."

The captain came in, grabbed his shirt from his desk and started buttoning it furiously. His phone rang and he snatched it up and barked into it, "*Ne?*" Gradually his face went pale and he sat slowly in his chair. I had taken the grinning Gallin to the sofa and sat with her.

"Gallin, I need you to listen very, very carefully. Everybody thinks you're dead. Including your father. You need to make a phone call—"

"To Dad, you're right."

"No, to the chief of the Mossad, or better still, if you have his number, the prime minister of Israel. We are on the clock, and they need to know two things, really soon. One, that you're alive, and two, that the Iranian missiles have been destroyed. You understand? Do it now!"

She stared at me a moment while the pieces fell into place. Then she went pale. "Holy shit!"

I handed her my phone and she dialed furiously.

———

SIX HUNDRED AND fifty miles away, south and west, the prime minister of Israel was standing in a small bunker deep beneath the Matcal Tower in Tel Aviv. He was accompanied by the Lt. General Chief of the General Staff, the Major General Deputy Chief and the Commanders of the Navy, the Ground Forces and the Air Force.

In the bunker also were a number of lower ranks seated at computer terminals. One of these spoke to the Lt. General Chief of the General Staff, who nodded and turned to the prime minister. "We are ready, Prime Minister. If you will say the precise words, 'Launch the rockets,' the operation will begin."

He swallowed hard, took a deep breath, said a prayer to God and said, "Launch the..." and at that very instant his cell rang. He hesitated; like a man drowning, clutching at one last straw, he said, "Excuse me," and pulled his cell from his pocket.

"Yes, who is this?"

The voice that spoke to him was dear to him, beloved,

but for a moment he wondered if he were losing his mind; for he had never expected to hear that voice again. It said, "Uncle! It's me, Aila! Is it too late? Is it too late, Uncle?"

He shook his head and staggered back into a chair. "No, no, but you...! You are dead!"

"Come on, Uncle! Get a grip! Listen to me! Did you trigger operation Ezekiel?"

"Not yet. You phoned..."

"Listen to me..."

He listened as she spoke, closed his eyes and heaved an enormous sigh of relief. He waved his hand at the Chief of the General Staff and mouthed "cancel, cancel!"

———

BACK IN ESENDERE, I stood and left Gallin talking on the phone to her uncle, the prime minister (who knew!) and approached the captain, who had just hung up from speaking to the foreign minister in Ankara. The captain looked up at me with a touch of fear and, I liked to think, a little awe.

I said, "Stand up, Captain."

The captain stood.

"Captain, I am in a hurry and I do not want to complicate my life today. So I am not going to shoot you or castrate you. But you should know that those are my two favored punishments for uniformed bastards who abuse their authority and rape women."

The captain stared at me. I put the full weight of my body into the right hook, which lifted the captain off his feet and hurled him a good ten feet diagonally across the room, where he lay motionless. I turned back and saw that Gallin had hung up and was smiling at me.

"You're a mensch," she said.

"I am?"

"Mm-hmm." She held up the phone. "You didn't read my WhatsApp."

"That was from you? I didn't read it, no. I was kind of busy."

"So how'd you know I was here?"

I shrugged. "Because it was you. It's what you would do."

"I guess I owe you dinner, at least."

I nodded. "At the very least."

EPILOGUE

"OK," she said, "so explain."

We had had dinner and now we were sitting on the sofa, sipping a fine Macallan in front of the fire. She had her head on a cushion and her bare feet on my knees, and was wiggling her toes.

I took a deep breath. "Where to begin?"

"The beginning is usually a good place," she said in a comfortable, sleepy voice.

"Well the story begins, if it has a beginning, shortly before the interglacial, when the Anunnaki came to Earth in Sumeria."

"Not that beginning. The other one."

"Oh. Well, there was this guy called Abraham..."

"I get the idea, Mason, our problems have no beginning and probably no end, but I am not too sleepy to slap you round the head. Now, explain."

Another deep breath and I gave it some thought. "Well, I guess the heart of the problem was that the people who betrayed you were not traitors. They believed passionately in the cause of Israel. Nothing was more important to them than the survival of Israel. And your enemies, in this case the Shiite Muslims in the form of Iran, believed even more passionately that nothing was more important than the destruction of Israel."

"That much I knew," she said with her eyes closed. "What about these people who betrayed me, us…? What was that all about? I mean, *Aaron?* Seriously?"

"I'm coming to that. So, for many, many years, decades, Israel has not only lived with the existential threat of hostile states on every border, and, as Aaron pointed out to me, in her very midst! She has also lived with the threat of nuclear devastation from Iran. And the fact that the reality of that threat rises and falls almost capriciously depending on which president happens to be in office in the States. Bush or Trump, the threat diminishes. Obama or Biden, the threat rises."

She nodded sleepily. "Because some presidents are serious about sanctions for nuclear research, and others aren't."

"And the Israelis don't even get to elect those presidents, but their national security depends on them."

"OK, so I still knew all this. When do we get to the chase?"

I took a slug of whisky and massaged her foot for a while.

"So most Israelis have learned to live with this situation, but some, intelligence officers subjected to the constant, unrelenting threat of imminent annihilation, began to feel that this was not a sustainable situation. They saw, rightly or wrongly, that sooner or later something was going to slip through the Iron Dome, and it might just be a weapon of mass destruction."

Her eyes opened. She didn't say anything. She just watched me. I went on.

"I met a few of them. Aaron was one, passionate, devoted, a good man who had been pushed too far. Marion, a guy with a beard whose name I never knew, yet I broke his jaw."

"That would make it hard to tell you his name."

I smiled, ruefully. "And then there was Colonel Paul Cohen."

"I'd heard of him. I'd never met him. He was stationed in New York, liaised with the Feds and the CIA." She shook her head. "He had a reputation. He was one hundred percent solid."

"Well, you know, little one, sometimes great strength lies in flexibility, and great weakness in inflexibility."

"You are so wise, sifu."

"I am, as you say, so wise. Anyhow, our Colonel Paul Cohen discovered that Iran was very, very close—much closer than anyone had up to that point believed—to making a bomb. Colonel Cohen, warrior that he was, saw this not as a threat, but as an opportunity."

Eyes closed again, she wagged a negative finger at me. "Explain that."

"The way of the intercepting fist. Your opponent pulls back his right fist and lunges forward, swinging wide for maximum power. What is this?"

"OK, an opportunity to lay out your opponent for good."

"Exactly. Step in quick and *bam*! Now, if your opponent is just swinging his fist, you knock him cold. But if his swinging an axe, or a knife..."

"You smash his windpipe, break his arm and then his neck."

"Did you ever consider writing poetry?"

She frowned with her eyes closed. "No."

"Good. So Colonel Cohen saw it the same way. But he knew that Israel and the States would probably both take steps to sabotage the nuclear program—"

"Wait, you're getting ahead of yourself. How did Cohen discover that Iran was so far advanced in the nuclear program?"

"He had an agent in there. An Italian-America rocket scientist by the name of Dr. Enzo Benini. Enzo Benini was sending Cohen regular reports updating him on the AEOI's progress. From the messages that have been recovered, it looks like Benini was getting ever more worried at Cohen's lack of action. But now we know the reason for that."

"We do," she said, then opened one eye. "We do? Talk me through it."

"Going back to the simile of the guy who's going to hit you, Cohen didn't want to simply knock Iran out."

"He wanted to smash its windpipe, break its arm and then its neck."

"Precisely, and for that he needed a credible excuse. The problem was, Benini became so worried, when he saw that launch day was approaching and Cohen wasn't doing anything, he became careless. His last message, a desperate plea for Cohen to act, was intercepted and Benini was murdered. So Cohen's next problem was to prevent the

Mossad from sending in a saboteur. He had recruited Aaron early on, knowing that he felt the same way about Iran. Aaron alerted him that you were taking the job and they set up the interviews with Ahmed."

"Wait..."

"Yes, Ahmed was Colonel Paul Cohen. They sold you out to Hezbollah via Sir Leo D'Arcy. You were abducted and taken to the Lebanese Embassy, and from there to Iran using diplomatic immunity."

She sat up and removed her feet from my lap, tucking them under her in a kind of half-lotus.

"Son of a bitch! So the plan all along was not to avoid Iran nuking us. It was to let them get as close as possible and then be justified in nuking them first in a preemptive strike."

"The way of the intercepting fist. Exactly. And it almost worked."

"Holy..."

"Yeah, it almost hit the holy fan. Aaron took his own life, and the NYPD found Cohen in his car on Lafayette Avenue, by Soundview Park, in the Bronx. He'd shot himself in the head."

"Allegedly."

"I guess."

Now she narrowed her eyes. "So, OK, when Nero discovered via the Institute that I had been abducted—"

"Everyone assumed you'd been murdered."

"We'll come to that. You were given the job I had originally applied for."

"Yup." I took a swig and savored it. "But because I was coming through ODIN instead of the Mossad, I was not intercepted by Cohen. My application went to Sir Leo

D'Arcy. And that was one of the first things that alerted me to the fact that something was wrong."

"But you were ordered to leave my disappearance up to the Israelis."

"Strictly."

"Very strictly."

She grinned. "But you ignored those orders."

"Totally, at risk of losing my career and my life."

"Huh, go figure."

"And after Aaron tried to kill me—"

"Aaron, Marion and David—"

"Was that his name?"

"You laid 'em all out. That was pretty cool. I didn't know you had it in you."

"As I was saying, after that it became pretty clear to me that this group had a vested interest in keeping your abduction secret. And when you thought it through, that meant they didn't want the Iranian missiles sabotaged. They were loyal agents, so there could only be one explanation. Trouble is, nobody wanted to listen to me."

"OK, I have two last questions."

"Shoot."

"With Enzo Benini dead, how the hell was Cohen going to know when to strike?"

"The answer to that comes in two parts. First, in collaboration with the Feds, they were keeping a tight watch on a Hezbollah cell in the Bronx. They knew from Benini that just before the strike, Hezbollah were going to make a diversionary strike in the USA, with a view to damaging American public support for Israel, and they were also going to trigger a massive rocket attack from Lebanon. Hezbollah have thousand of rockets stashed in Lebanon for that very purpose."

"I know that, Mason. It still seems to me very risky for a plan that depended so much on very precise timing."

"There was something else. MI6 also had a man in there. The AEOI's nuclear program was a Gruyère cheese, riddled with moles."

"Your metaphor went a bit awry there, Mason."

"But you get the idea. This guy had been on the inside for about a year. Got in via Sir Leo D'Arcy, and had been assisting Enzo Benini. He was posing as a Danish expert in propulsion systems. Nice guy."

"You left him at the lab when it blew?"

"When *I* blew it, you mean? No, he slipped away in Esendere, while we were chatting with the captain. He was shy. So, you said you had two more questions. You get one more and then I'm going to get the caramelized pears marinated in cognac and topped with fresh whipped cream and flaked almonds."

She made a smug face I couldn't quite read and lay back on the sofa and put her feet on my knees again. Then she sipped her whisky and said:

"How did you know I was in Chalus?"

"Oh, that's easy. The guy who ran the facility, the chief administrator, was a guy called Mr. Abdul. I took him down to the rocketry lab to help me blow the place. Before I launched the rockets, I rolled him on his back, knelt on his chest and pressed the muzzle of the semiautomatic I had taken from one of the guards, into his right knee. Then I told him that if he didn't tell me..."

"No, no, tell it properly. Like it happened."

"OK, I *snarled* at him, 'Lie to me and I will blow your knee in half.' He whimpered,

'No, please, anything, anything, I tell you anything! So I growled, 'The English woman who was arrested as a spy, where was she taken?'" She wasn't so much laughing as gurgling. I shrugged. "So he told me you'd been taken to Chalus, on the Caspian Sea, and you had been interrogated by a senior specialist officer, but that you had escaped."

"And what did you think."

"C'mon!"

"Go on, tell me."

"I thought that was just about typical of you, and I figured, knowing you..."

"You do know me, don't you."

"Yeah. I figured, knowing you, you'd steal a car and make for Esendere."

"What else did you think? Did you think I was amazing?"

"Get outta here! Come on, pears, cognac and cream!"

And we went arm-in-arm to the kitchen.

Don't miss ASSETS AND LIABILITIES. The riveting sequel in the Alex Mason Thriller series.

Scan the QR code below to purchase ASSETS AND LIABILITIES.

Or go to: righthouse.com/assets-and-liabilities

NOTE: flip to the very end to read an exclusive sneak peak...

DON'T MISS ANYTHING!

If you want to stay up to date on all new releases in this series, with these authors, or with any of our new deals, you can do so by joining our newsletters below.

In addition, you will immediately gain access to our entire *Right House VIP Library,* which currently includes *ORIGINS*—a full length prequel novel to *ODIN.*

righthouse.com/email

(Easy to unsubscribe. No spam. Ever.)

ALSO BY DAVID ARCHER

Executive Order (Book 6)
Dead Man Talking (Book 7)
All The King's Men (Book 8)
Flashpoint (Book 9)
Brotherhood of the Goat (Book 10)
Dead Hot (Book 11)
Blood on Megiddo (Book 12)
Son of Hell (Book 13)

NOAH WOLF THRILLERS
Code Name Camelot (Book 1)
Lone Wolf (Book 2)
In Sheep's Clothing (Book 3)
Hit for Hire (Book 4)
The Wolf's Bite (Book 5)
Black Sheep (Book 6)
Balance of Power (Book 7)
Time to Hunt (Book 8)
Red Square (Book 9)
Highest Order (Book 10)
Edge of Anarchy (Book 11)
Unknown Evil (Book 12)
Black Harvest (Book 13)
World Order (Book 14)
Caged Animal (Book 15)
Deep Allegiance (Book 16)
Pack Leader (Book 17)
High Treason (Book 18)
A Wolf Among Men (Book 19)
Rogue Intelligence (Book 20)
Alpha (Book 21)

Rogue Wolf (Book 22)
Shadows of Allegiance (Book 23)
In the Grip of Darkness (Book 24)

SAM PRICHARD MYSTERIES
The Grave Man (Book 1)
Death Sung Softly (Book 2)
Love and War (Book 3)
Framed (Book 4)
The Kill List (Book 5)
Drifter: Part One (Book 6)
Drifter: Part Two (Book 7)
Drifter: Part Three (Book 8)
The Last Song (Book 9)
Ghost (Book 10)
Hidden Agenda (Book 11)

SAM AND INDIE MYSTERIES
Aces and Eights (Book 1)
Fact or Fiction (Book 2)
Close to Home (Book 3)
Brave New World (Book 4)
Innocent Conspiracy (Book 5)
Unfinished Business (Book 6)
Live Bait (Book 7)
Alter Ego (Book 8)
More Than It Seems (Book 9)
Moving On (Book 10)
Worst Nightmare (Book 11)
Chasing Ghosts (Book 12)
Serial Superstition (Book 13)

ALSO BY BLAKE BANNER

Up to date books can be found at:
www.righthouse.com/blake-banner

ROGUE THRILLERS
Gates of Hell (Book 1)
Hell's Fury (Book 2)

ALEX MASON THRILLERS
Odin (Book 1)
Ice Cold Spy (Book 2)
Mason's Law (Book 3)
Assets and Liabilities (Book 4)
Russian Roulette (Book 5)
Executive Order (Book 6)
Dead Man Talking (Book 7)
All The King's Men (Book 8)
Flashpoint (Book 9)
Brotherhood of the Goat (Book 10)
Dead Hot (Book 11)
Blood on Megiddo (Book 12)
Son of Hell (Book 13)

HARRY BAUER THRILLER SERIES
Dead of Night (Book 1)
Dying Breath (Book 2)
The Einstaat Brief (Book 3)

Quantum Kill (Book 4)
Immortal Hate (Book 5)
The Silent Blade (Book 6)
LA: Wild Justice (Book 7)
Breath of Hell (Book 8)
Invisible Evil (Book 9)
The Shadow of Ukupacha (Book 10)
Sweet Razor Cut (Book 11)
Blood of the Innocent (Book 12)
Blood on Balthazar (Book 13)
Simple Kill (Book 14)
Riding The Devil (Book 15)
The Unavenged (Book 16)
The Devil's Vengeance (Book 17)
Bloody Retribution (Book 18)
Rogue Kill (Book 19)
Blood for Blood (Book 20)

DEAD COLD MYSTERY SERIES
An Ace and a Pair (Book 1)
Two Bare Arms (Book 2)
Garden of the Damned (Book 3)
Let Us Prey (Book 4)
The Sins of the Father (Book 5)
Strange and Sinister Path (Book 6)
The Heart to Kill (Book 7)
Unnatural Murder (Book 8)
Fire from Heaven (Book 9)
To Kill Upon A Kiss (Book 10)
Murder Most Scottish (Book 11)

ABOUT US

Right House is an independent publisher created by authors for readers. We specialize in Action, Thriller, Mystery, and Crime novels.

If you enjoyed this novel, then there is a good chance you will like what else we have to offer! Please stay up to date by using any of the links below.

Join our mailing lists to stay up to date -->
righthouse.com/email
Visit our website --> righthouse.com
Contact us --> contact@righthouse.com

 facebook.com/righthousebooks
X x.com/righthousebooks
instagram.com/righthousebooks

EXCLUSIVE SNEAK PEAK OF...

ASSETS AND LIABILITIES

PROLOGUE

Mira Finn was uncharacteristically cold-blooded for an Irishwoman.

It was the kind of 20th-century, racist, misogynistic comment Nero, the director of ODIN, was fond of making while stuffing his face with gourmet food and drink. It didn't bother her. She tended to agree. Most of the Irish people she had grown up with in Dublin had been pretty hot-blooded, the women more than the men. She had never understood why they got so excited, far less the things they got excited about: clean socks, clean knickers, a clean front room. Cleanliness was generally involved. She didn't feel anything about cleanliness. She didn't feel anything about most things.

She selected one of several prepaid cell phones which she had bought the day before at Start Marais on Rue Vieille de Temple. She dialed a number she had been given. It rang three times and a man's voice spoke with a French accent.

"Hallo, who is calling, please?"

"Is that Amazon deliveries? I'm phoning about a package I am supposed to receive today. I wonder if I could change the delivery location."

"Yes, of course. Where would you like the package delivered?"

"Can you deliver it to Café Le Rostand, Place Edmond Rostand?"

"No problem, madame. Shall I deliver it at the bar?"

"No, I'll be sitting on the terrace with a copy of the *New York Herald Tribune* on the table. Four o'clock this afternoon."

A brief snort. "*Le Carré vit encore*. Sixteen hour."

The voice hung up.

Mira showered, changed her clothes and at three PM went for a stroll down Boulevard Saint-Michel as far as the Port Royal metro station. There she bought a Herald Tribune and made her way back up the boulevard to the café, where she sat outside in the early spring sunshine, ordered a glass of cold white wine and settled to read the paper. It was three forty-five.

At five minutes past four a dark Audi pulled up. The passenger door opened and a man with very short hair and a leather jacket climbed out. As the man moved in among the tables, the car pulled away to park farther up the road. Mira watched the man approach her table. He smiled. He spoke with an American accent.

"Good afternoon. Do you mind if I join you?"

"Actually I am expecting someone."

"I think I am the man you're expecting. The Amazon delivery guy?"

She felt nothing, but had a momentary flash of Nero

calling her cold-blooded. "I have no idea what you are talking about. But you are intruding on my privacy, so I would thank you to move along."

He gave a small laugh. "No need to get touchy. We actually need to talk."

He pulled out the chair and sat. She watched him do it and still felt nothing like fear or panic, though she knew perhaps she should.

"I wouldn't recommend telling the waiter to get rid of me, or calling the cops. You really do need to hear what I have to say."

"Who are you?"

He smiled. "You can call me Joe. I am a friend of Peter's."

"Peter?"

The smile faded from his face. "You are waiting for Peter, right?"

She sighed and glanced at the waiter, wondering what her next move should be.

"Look, uh, Joe. Either you're out of your mind or you have mistaken me for somebody else. Either way you're spoiling my afternoon. So I am going to ask you to move along."

He reached in his pocket and pulled out a cell phone which he placed on the table in front of her. An audio file began to play.

"'Hallo, who is calling, please?' 'Is that Amazon deliveries? I'm phoning about a package I am supposed to receive today. I wonder if I could change the delivery location.' 'Yes, of course. Where would you like the package delivered?' 'Can you deliver it to Café Le Rostand, Place Edmond

Rostand?' 'No problem, madame. Shall I deliver it at the bar?' 'No, I'll be sitting on the terrace with a copy of the New York Herald Tribune on the table. Four o'clock this afternoon.' 'Le Carré vit encore. Sixteen hour.'"

It stopped and Joe reached over and retrieved the phone. He didn't say anything. He seemed to search for something on his cell, then pressed the screen with his thumb, and a moment later her burner began to ring in her bag. He smiled at her. "Oops! I really think we need to talk, Ms Finn."

Three people in the world, aside from her, knew why she was in Paris. They had deliberately done it that way. The president of the United States knew she was there and why. Nero, the Director of ODIN, and the man he described as his most trusted agent, Alex Mason. Nobody else was supposed to know.

She looked across the road at the Luxembourg Gardens. There was a growing warmth in her gut. She didn't know whether it was fear or rage, but it was a powerful feeling. She spoke quietly.

"You lay one finger on me and I will kick and scream and claw until the waiters drag you off me, by which time we will have cops crawling all over this café like flies over a dead Russian. I suggest you take your phone and mince your tight little fanny out of here, Joe, before we end up causing an international incident."

He nodded. "OK." He thumbed the cell, called a number and muttered something, then hung up and slipped the phone into his inside pocket. When his hand reemerged it was holding a leather wallet. Out of the corner of her eye Mira saw the dark Audi backing down the street, emitting a high whine. As it drew level Joe stood, holding the open wallet high in the air with his left hand, shouting, "Gendarmerie Nationale! Gendarmerie Nationale!"

In his right hand he had a gun. He fired once into the air. Suddenly everybody was screaming and running. The doors of the Audi were flung open and three large, athletic men were descending on her.

She screamed, smashed her wineglass and stabbed hard at Joe's face with it. He bellowed with rage and she shouldered past him at a run, but ran straight into three men the size of small redwood trees. They scooped her up and carried her kicking and screaming across the sidewalk and bundled her into the back of the Audi, while the waiters and the customers at the café looked on and wondered what to do. Joe climbed into the front passenger seat pressing a white napkin to his torn face. The napkin was rapidly turning red. "Gendarmerie Nationale!" he shouted one more time, and the car accelerated away with a squeal of tires.

Nobody took the number of the license plate.

Sprawled across the two men on the back seat, Mira felt a sharp stab in her ass, and for a moment felt intense emotion. Her belly burned and she was aware of an intense need to leave the car. She heard the engine accelerate, tried to move and found she could not.

———

THE NEXT THING she was aware of was a feeling of nausea. As her eyes opened she found she was in the dark. Her hands hurt badly and so did her feet. She tried to move them but could not. She was sitting, and as awareness returned in the blackness, she realized she was tied to a chair. For a moment her cold blood became ice, and a moment later it was molten terror.

She had no idea how long she waited. Time has no meaning in absolute blackness. But by the time she heard the key turning in the padlock she had been through screaming rage, sobbing grief, pleading fear and numbness.

When the doors opened she found she was in a steel container of the sort used to transport goods on trucks and ships. A spotlight glared in her eyes, blinding her, and she turned away, squeezing her eyes tight. When she opened them again it was to find she was in a dentist's chair. Her hands and her feet were purple and swollen from having been tied too tight too long, with mountaineering bootlaces.

A silhouette appeared in the doorway, slightly amorphous against the bright light outside. He seemed to be carrying something in his hands. It was a small, metal table and it rattled as he set it down. He pulled on some surgical gloves and stepped closer to her, leaning forward with his hands on his knees. She realized there must be a bulb above her head, because a halo of dull light illuminated his features. His eyes were squinting. His mouth, framed by a scraggy moustache and beard, was slightly open and creased into a smile.

"Are we wakey-wake?"

"Please don't do this. This is not necessary."

He laughed. It was an ugly chortle. He held up a large, crumpled ball of blue and white linen.

"You know what is this?"

She gave her head a minute shake. She was aware her heart was racing and she felt sick.

"Is butcher's apron."

He turned and walked away, morphing into a hazy form in the glow of the spotlight as he slipped the apron over his head. Her mind was racing too fast for her to hold on to the thoughts. Her mind was full of a screaming voice telling her it could not find a solution.

Another form appeared in the door and walked toward her with slow steps. When he spoke his accent was American.

"It looks like you're in a lot of trouble, Mira."

"Just tell me what you want. I am not a hero."

"That's good to know."

"I swear, I will do anything."

"OK."

He moved to the side and returned with a chair. He sat and his face came into the halo of light. She went very cold inside. It was a cold that was beyond ice. It vanquished all hope. He smiled.

"This changes things a bit, doesn't it, Mira?"

All she could think to say was, "What do you want?"

"I want to know who ODIN's contacts are in Moscow."

"I know some of them. Only Nero knows all of them. But I can find out."

"Good. Recite the ones you know. This is being recorded. But, Mira—" He paused. "Do remember that if you lie, we will find out."

"I won't lie."

And as she said it, grief, shame and humiliation made her weep. She spoke, and once she had started she could not stop. She gave him everything she knew, including the whereabouts of Peter Rusenko, the Amazon packet she was supposed to collect, and the contacts who were supposed to bring him to her.

When she was done the man went to stand. She said, "Wait! There is more."

"More?"

"I can be of use to you. Nobody has ever penetrated ODIN. Send me back. I am trusted. I can supply you with information from the highest levels. I can keep you posted on practically every ODIN operation that is executed."

He frowned with his eyebrows and smiled with his lips, then sat back and crossed one leg over the other.

"Seriously? What do you think your worth will be to ODIN once Rusenko is captured, tried and executed?"

"Don't! Let me take him in. My stock will rise in ODIN, I can get closer to Nero, and at the same time I can run Rusenko. I will tailor what information he gives the Americans, and channel information from him back to you about what projects they have him working on."

He chuckled. "How stupid do you think I am, Mira? You really think I am going to let you go through with your original plan?"

A small ember of hope began to glow in her belly.

"Yes, I admit, it's a ploy for you to set me free and get out of this with all my limbs and my life intact. But think about it. You are still in time. Right now, in this moment, you own one of ODIN's top operatives. How often are you going to get that opportunity? You can destroy me any time you like. I have no choice but to do everything you tell me. And not only that, you are going to have one of Russia's leading scientists positioned within an American defense program, handled by me. OK, it's a ploy for me to get out of here alive. But it also happens to be a golden opportunity for you."

The smirk slowly evaporated from his face and his eyes became distracted. He pulled a pack of Camels from his pocket, pinched one free and lit up. He sat there, thinking, inhaling the smoke deep into his lungs until the cigarette was practically down to the filter. Then he looked at Mira, thrust out his bottom lip and nodded. The ember of hope in her belly sprouted flames, but she fought not to show it. The man stood and walked out into the glow from the spotlight. For a moment nothing happened. Then another shadow morphed through the glare. It was the leering form of the man in the butcher's apron.

From where he stood at the door to the warehouse, the American heard the scream. It was a horrible, inhuman sound. Worse. It was the sound of a living being losing its humanity. Somewhere, deep inside, a residual part of him was glad the United States no longer did this kind of thing. But he also recognized this was the very reason Russia was growing in strength and would soon be swarming all over Europe, while the pussies in NATO peed in their frilly panties and developed non-lethal weapons. The game goes to the meanest son of a bitch in the valley. That was a lesson he had learned a long time ago.

———

DAWN CAME GRAY AND COLD. On the Ile de la Cité, between the Pont Notre-Dame and the Pont d'Arcole, gray, granite steps descended to the frigid water opposite the Hôtel-Dieu. Trash and green slime tended to accumulate around the base of those steps. So it was past seven thirty before anybody noticed that among the slime and the trash there was something else. A green blouse was pointed out by one person to another. Then dark jeans were spotted, and finally red hair that moved softly on the ripples of the water. The river police were the first to dispatch a unit, and it was they who found that it was a young woman who had been cruelly mutilated.

Half an hour later the BRI—the Brigade de Recherche et d'Intervention—had cordoned off that section of the Quai de la Corse, and the steps down to the river. Blue lights flashed and pulsed in the dull morning against the gray stone walls and on the gray murk of the Seine.

The medical examiner had made his preliminary examination on the lower steps, by the water. Then the body had been carried with difficulty up to the sidewalk, where they had zipped it into a body bag before wheeling it into the ambulance. Then the blue, pulsing lights had started mournfully to disperse. Some of them returned to police headquarters, and others to the morgue.

CHAPTER 1

Lovelock had called me at noon from a burner, which was unusual. Lovelock called always from the office on the secure line. She had given me verbal instructions in less than thirty seconds and hung up without allowing me to reply. The instructions were not so much complicated as convoluted. So much so that I had written them down as soon as she had hung up, in order to give myself time to memorize them properly.

It had involved going for a walk to McMillan Park and then continuing on to Columbia Heights where I would get the Metro to Chinatown, switch trains and go to L'Enfant Plaza where I had to switch again to the Metro Center, return to Gallery Place in Chinatown and travel north to U Street.

After that, if I was satisfied I had not been followed, I was to take a circuitous route, on foot, via V Street and T Street, to Vernon Street, to a safe house we had there.

It was unusual. But then, I told myself, Nero was

nothing if not a man of contradictions. On the one hand he was obsessive about routine and detested change, yet he was one of the most unpredictable men I had ever met. The key was of course that his attacks of unpredictability tended to affect *other* people's routines, not his.

This time, once again, was different.

The house on Vernon Street was a small, Georgian redbrick with a sage green door at the top of thirteen steps. I was vaguely aware as I climbed them that thirteen steps in DC generally suggested some historical connection with the Man Himself and those who had laid the foundation stones of the New Atlantis.

I knocked on the door and it was opened by a man I had never seen before. To say he appeared aloof would be like saying the Antarctic was chilly. He had a nose a hawk would envy, eyebrows that could look down on their own forehead, a white chef's coat and a regal bearing to shame kings. He gazed at me like I was an insult and he was awaiting my apology. Following Lovelock's instructions I said, "Did you advertise a dining table for sale?"

He groaned softly as he sighed and replied, "We 'ave only a Queen Anne, perraps it is too refined for monsieur."

"Queen Anne will do fine."

"*Eh bien*, please, come in." He stepped back and closed the door behind me. "Follow me, *s'il vous plaît*."

I followed him across a tiled floor to a door on the left. He knocked with the back of his knuckle, stared at the ceiling until Nero's voice called, "Enter!" and opened the door for me.

I was not surprised to find myself in a dining room. There was a long, mahogany table. Nero considered tablecloths vulgar and middle class, so he had two placemats. He was at the head of the table with a view of the heavy, burgundy drapes that had been drawn across the window. A fire burned in a Georgian, marble fireplace and there was a bottle of white wine open in a bucket of ice on the table.

Nero did not stand. He nudged his knife with his fingernail and said, "You're late."

"I was escaping from ghosts. Besides, you didn't give a time."

"Sit down. I assume you haven't eaten."

"Manny Pacquiao is eating my beef ragout as we speak."

He stared at me blankly. "The boxer?"

"My cat."

"We have a turbot mousse and salmon mousse with a nice Gewürztraminer." As he said it he tucked a large linen napkin into his collar. "After that we have lamb broiled in honey and eucalyptus, with a nice 2016 Chateau Clinet. As I am sure you know, 2016 was a superb year in Bordeaux."

"You had mentioned it."

"Are you going to sit down, or do you intend to eat standing up, like one of those people one sees outside Metro stations?"

I sat and draped my napkin on my left knee. He extracted the bottle from the ice and poured me a glass.

"Sir, I believe this is one of the very few times I have ever seen you outside your office. And though we have eaten in the same room before, this is the first time you have invited me to lunch."

"Your point being that these two exceptional circumstances imply an exceptional cause."

"Yes, and also, why the very convoluted meeting? Couldn't I have simply gone to the office, as I always do?"

"No. Clearly not."

The door opened and the man with the enviable nose delivered two plates, each containing two mousse, one pink and one white. He delivered also a basket of crackers, and refilled our glasses. Nero waved his fingers at him in a "go away" sort of gesture.

"Thank you, Lucas. I'll call you when we are ready."

Lucas bowed and left.

"How do you manage to stay in the nineteenth century without getting caught and sent back?"

He looked at me with a trace of a smile but didn't answer.

"Alex, ODIN is seriously compromised." I spread salmon mousse on a cracker and waited for him to go on. "Mira was caught. Her body was pulled from the Seine yesterday morning. She had been badly tortured. We must assume she told them everything she knew."

"How much did she know?"

"Too much, but that, as it turns out, is the least of our worries." He waved his hand at my starter and said, "Enjoy in silence while I fill you in. You can ask questions later."

We chewed a moment. He sipped and went on.

"Now, facts, Dr. Rusenko is on the run. I received a very brief telephone call from him the day before yesterday at three PM Paris time. He said that he had not received the call he was expecting from Mira Finn. Yet, a little earlier we had received confirmation from her that contact had been made and she was going to arrange a meeting. Correct codes had been used. When we attempted to contact Mira she could not be found, and her telephone seemed to be turned off."

"Did you send someone to look for her?"

"As you know agents have operational discretion as far as is possible. It was down to her to arrange the handover point, and it was essential that as few people as possible knew where that would be. In this case, in theory, it was Mira, Rusenko and his Paris contact. Had she checked in as she was supposed to, then I would have known too. But she didn't. We later found out from the BRI—"

"The BRI?"

"The *Brigade de Recherche et d'Intervention*," he said in an annoyingly perfect French accent, "that a woman fitting Mira's description had been abducted from the Café Le Rostand, on the Place Edmond Rostand. The café is a twenty-minute walk from her apartment and would have been a suitable place for the handover. It remains unclear what prevented her from communicating to me where the handover would take place."

"Description of the abductors?"

"Dark Audi, four large, fit men in jeans and leather jackets, claiming to be policemen. They pulled her from her table and forced her into the back of the vehicle, then took off south. That of course gives us no indication whatever of where they took her."

"Sir, this raises some pretty tough questions."

"Indeed."

"Correct me if I am wrong, but to the best of my knowledge, very few people knew Mira was in Paris, and only four knew why. If the Russians knew that Mira was there to collect Dr. Rusenko, it means that one of those four people told them."

"You are absolutely correct, Alex. The fact that Rusenko did not receive the communication from her, the fact that I did not receive her call, and the fact that she was snatched from an obvious handover point all suggest that her phone had been compromised, and that they knew she was there to receive Rusenko." He wagged his knife. "But here is a thing: They did *not* know where Rusenko was, or how to get to him. Remember, Rusenko is a highly intelligent man. He enjoys Le Carré and Len Deighton in the original English and does the *Daily Telegraph* cryptic crossword every morning in ten to fifteen minutes."

I stared at him blankly for a moment. "So, they took her to find out where he was, but he had already been alerted by not hearing from her, and he vanished." I scratched my head. "But why not allow her to make the call to Rusenko, set up the meet and snatch them both?"

"Because, I imagine, they feared that once Mira and Rusenko made contact, that would be communicated to us along with the handover location and we and the CIA would be all over them. They hoped that by snatching her they might be able to find out his whereabouts and snatch him before we could respond."

I nodded and drained my glass. As I set it down I said, "OK, that makes sense. So we are left looking for the leak. And the leak has to be either you, General Patrick O'Connor, the president of the United States or me."

"That is about the size of it, Alex, yes."

The door opened and Lucas brought in a dish of lamb, which he uncovered and proceeded to carve and serve on a bed of potatoes fried in olive oil and garlic and garnished with absolutely nothing because it didn't need it, and nobody present was likely to be offended by the absence of lettuce.

Lucas poured the wine and withdrew. We ate in reverent silence for a while. Eventually Nero pointed at the lamb and spoke with his mouth full.

"Lucas. He cooks this. He is very good."

I nodded and, a while later, I drained my glass and slid it across the table to him.

"So, as I understand it, I have two objectives."

He refilled our glasses and muttered, "Tell me."

"Find Rusenko before the Russians do, and find the leak."

"Well, the leak is fairly obvious. Your objective is a little more complex than you see it."

"The leak is obvious?"

"I can see I need to draw you a picture, Alex. Objectively —and the only people in this situation capable of being truly objective are you and I—objectively the leak is easy to iden-tify. However, from the president's perspective, and from General O'Connor's perspective, it is equally obvious who the leak is."

I sat back and picked up my glass. "You're going to have to spell it out, sir."

"The leak is either General O'Connor, or the president. The president is very unlikely because at his level of power things are done differently. However, General O'Connor might well be in the pay of Moscow. He is an able man and he is an advisor to the president, but he has been passed over a couple of times for high-prestige posts and he harbors resentment against colleagues and former administrations. If Putin offered him enough, he might well take the bait.

"However, that being the case, he would need a scapegoat." He stared at me for a long moment and I felt my skin going cold. He nodded. "Yes, Alex, you are the scapegoat. I had intended to make you a part of this mission because you are my best man, but he specifically requested you be part of the team anyway. He had you lined up to take the fall from the start."

"So, sir, am I under arrest? Is that why I am here?"

"Don't be absurd. You are here because we need to hammer out the details of your mission. Your first priority is to find Dr. Rusenko and deliver him to ODIN. Your second objective is to establish precisely where the leak is, and uncover the chain of communication from the Kremlin to the White House. That chain will lead to O'Connor's accomplices and contacts in Washington. Aside from anything else, Alex, it is the only way to clear your name."

We finished the lamb and the wine in silence. When we were finished I wiped my mouth and dropped the napkin on the table.

"It will be very difficult for you to provide me with help."

"Very difficult indeed, Alex. However, before you go I shall provide you with a cell phone with which you can communicate with me. But you must keep that communication to an absolute minimum."

"Thank you, sir."

"I also have a file for you to study and some documents you can use, passport, et cetera. You will have to go to Paris, of course." He sighed. "Aside from that I am afraid you are pretty much on your own, and in any case it is probably preferable that I do not know what you are doing, or how you are going about it."

I nodded. "Understood."

"Now, some cheese, a little whiskey, and you had better be on your way."

AN HOUR later I left the safe house as the afternoon was turning to copper, and walked the four hundred yards to the Washington Hilton on Connecticut Avenue. There I checked in using the documents Nero had provided me with, and went up to my room to study the scant information he'd been able to give me. It was about forty percent fact and sixty percent opinion. On the plus side, when you got to know Nero, you realized that most of the time his opinion was worth more than the facts. I dined at the hotel, had an early night and, in the morning I took a cab to my bank on G Street, opposite the Metro Center Station.

When I climbed from the taxi, the air was fresh and early-morning cool in the shade of the trees. They might have been pin oaks, or maples, or London plane trees. I promised myself yet again, as I paced the sidewalk in the morning air, that when I had more time I would learn all the names of common trees and plants. So if I ever had grandchildren I could take them for informative country walks, and look wise.

A young woman appeared within the bank, hunkered down on the other side of the big, glass doors and unlocked them. I stopped pacing, grunted a quiet smile and told myself that my ever having grandchildren was about as likely as Nero becoming vegan and adopting "Namaste" as a greeting.

Once inside I had a quiet word with the cashier, who had a quiet word with an assistant manager who in turn had a quiet word with a security guard. Then the security guard and the assistant manager had a quiet word with me and took me quietly down some carpeted stairs to an elevator which descended a couple of floors to a red-carpeted basement that smelt of wax furniture polish. There, I was taken down a short passage to a small room with a steel door. The assistant manager and the security guard each had a key. They unlocked the door and stood aside while I went into the small vault to withdraw my safety deposit box.

Not all safety deposit boxes are that well guarded, but you get what you pay for, and I paid over the odds for this one. This had nothing to do with ODIN. They knew nothing about it. This was mine, one of several I had around the world, and I thought of it as an emergency survival kit.

It contained an attaché case with a hundred thousand dollars in untraceable bills, a passport in the name of Samuel Silver, a driver's license and a Mastercard Black. It also contained a sealed plastic bag with a fake moustache, hair dye, glasses and shaving equipment, just in case. There were other bits and pieces, like a couple of prepaid burners and some electronic toys, but mainly it was the basic essentials. I figured that if I was going to be on the run for a while, it was best not even ODIN knew who I was or where I was.

I checked the contents, snapped the case shut and left the bank to take a walk up 11ᵗʰ Street to the Starbucks at the Grand Hyatt. There I had a double espresso and a croissant, and used one of the burners to contact Aila Gallin in London.

"What?"

"Hello darling, I thought you'd be pleased to hear from me."

"Oh, it's you. It just said United States on the screen. I thought Microsoft was trying to sell me something again."

"Well, you know how it is, kiddo, we all have problems..."

I let the words linger and she caught them.

"Yeah? Anything I can do?"

"Oh, you know, it's the usual stuff. You're lucky, you have a very supportive family. I mean, I doubt they'd be interested in my problems. But my family? Man! They just leave me out in the cold."

"Holy shit! Are you serious?"

I laughed. "You know how it is. Your cousin upsets everybody and you end up getting the blame. But listen, I don't want to burden you with my woes."

"Don't be stupid. Can you make it to London?"

"Oh, that would be swell. Might be a couple of days. But just keep it between you and me, OK? I wouldn't want to offend Aunt Aggie."

"You got it. Call me and I'll collect you at the airport."

"You're a doll."

I hung up, left the warm smell of morning coffee and cakes and went out into the morning to hail a cab.

Scan the QR code below to purchase ASSETS AND LIABILITIES.

Or go to: righthouse.com/assets-and-liabilities

NOTES

CHAPTER 5

1. The Mossad